KEEP ME CLOSE

A Light My Fire Novel

J.H. CROIX

This is a work of fiction. Names, characters, businesses, places, events and incidents are either the products of the author's imagination or used in a fictitious manner. Any resemblance to actual persons, living or dead, or actual events is purely coincidental.

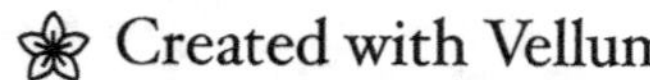 Created with Vellum

To those who took the detour when life created it.

Sign up for my newsletter for information on new releases & get a FREE copy of one of my books!

http://jhcroixauthor.com/subscribe/

Follow me!
jhcroix@jhcroix.com
https://amazon.com/author/jhcroix
https://www.bookbub.com/authors/j-h-croix
https://www.facebook.com/jhcroix
https://www.instagram.com/jhcroix/

HALLIE

My hands were curled so tightly around the steering wheel that my fingers hurt. When I finally let go, I sat there, trying to take a breath. My lungs felt tight, and my heart ached.

I was only thirty years old. That was it. I tried to tell myself it wasn't a big deal. The news could be worse. I was going to survive. I was going to be fine. *Fine.*

But, but—

I shook that thought away so hard it skittered off into the dark edges of my mind. Awareness clicked into place, and I finally noticed I was just sitting there in the parking lot at the grocery store.

Abruptly, I decided I didn't want to go

grocery shopping, not today. I didn't even want to go back to my lonely apartment tonight, but I didn't want to see anybody I knew. I wanted to pretend everything was fine. As if I hadn't just discussed when I'd be scheduling surgery.

I started my car again, stretching my hands before I began driving. I headed out of Anchorage, watching the city lights disappear in the darkness.

Moonlight gilded the snow-topped mountains with a silvery glow. I'd always loved how it felt as if the mountains cradled the city. They felt so close, as if I could reach out and touch them.

Though it was bracingly cold outside, it was clear, and the roads were plowed. I told myself I would just drive for a little bit, maybe stop at the first exit outside the city. I passed that exit, but I wasn't ready to stop yet. A while later when I saw the exit for Willow Brook, I smiled. I'd been here a few times. The downtown area had a cute little coffee shop. It was just far enough outside of Anchorage that I didn't come often. I typically drove south rather than west. My brother lived in Diamond Creek, another small town roughly five hours south.

I couldn't even remember why I'd come

to Willow Brook the last time. I thought it was because a friend had an art show in a gallery here. The town was just big enough that I could find somewhere to stay. When I turned onto Main Street and saw the sign for Wildlands Lodge & Restaurant, I whispered, "Here."

I could stay here, have a good dinner, and pretend my life belonged to someone else for the night.

I checked into my room and dropped off my backpack, which had some toiletries and a change of clothes. Not because I planned this night, but because I always had that in my car. You never knew what might happen when driving in winter weather in Alaska. That was a habit I'd carried since I was younger and more carefree and traveled frequently.

I glanced in the mirror before I left the bathroom and swiped a brush through my light-brown hair. My hazel eyes blinked at me behind my glasses. I slipped a tube of lip gloss out of my purse and smoothed it across my lips.

"There," I said to my reflection. "You look fine."

I looked nothing like I felt, as if I was cracking along the seams. I jogged down the wide stairs at the lodge. It was a nice place, with guest rooms in the two wings off the main section and a restaurant and bar downstairs. The lodge was situated on a lake with the lights from the dock glittering in the darkness. Tonight, the reflection from the moonlight shimmered on the surface of the frozen lake.

Moments later, I walked into the bar and restaurant and glanced around. It was busy, busier than I'd expected for winter. My guess was it was a favorite local hangout.

My eyes landed on the bar, and I strolled across the room, the heels of my cowboy boots striking the wide plank hardwood flooring. I ordered a sangria with a burger and fries.

I was starting to feel carefree. This was what I used to do—on a whim, go to new places by myself. You could be who you wanted to be because nobody knew you.

As I sipped my drink and looked around the crowded space, my eyes collided with a man's. He was leaning on the opposite corner of the bar from me. The lights from above glinted on his dark hair.

When his dark gaze connected with mine, it felt like a flame lit in the air, heat flickering across the distance between us. He was, as they say, tall, dark and handsome. My body buzzed, and I took a long swallow from my drink, casting a smile in his direction. His return smile was subtle, just a kick of his lips at one corner paired with a barely-there wink. It sent my belly in a swoop and a spin.

I swallowed and thought maybe, just maybe, I could forget everything for a night. I could pretend I was carefree and careless and reckless.

A few minutes later, the man rested his elbows on the bar beside me. "Hi," I said, injecting boldness into my tone.

He dipped his chin. "Hey there, I'm Chase."

"I'm Hallie."

"Nice to meet you, Hallie."

His voice was low and rumbly. It both invigorated and soothed my nerves. I'd never had a one-night stand, but I decided tonight was the night. It was perfect. *He* was perfect.

"I don't think you're from around here," he observed.

I shook my head. "I'm not. You must be."

He grinned. "I am. How long are you here?"

"Just tonight."

"Well, it's good to meet you."

I smiled up at him.

"I need to say hi to some friends. Are you going to be here much longer? Here, meaning the bar," he clarified.

I cocked my head to the side, angling to look up at him and wondering if I'd lost my mind. My gut told me he wasn't crazy or evil, and I was desperate for a thorough distraction to take my mind off my worries.

"Yes, I'm staying here tonight."

Another dip of his head as his dark eyes searched mine. "I'll be back then."

He moved to straighten and push away from the bar, and I reached out, catching him lightly by the elbow. He glanced down, arching a brow.

"Promise me you're a nice guy." As if a promise from a near-stranger would mean anything.

"I promise. You can ask the bartender. She'll vouch for me." He gestured toward a woman behind the bar.

She smiled over at us. "What is it?"

"Tell Hallie I'm a nice guy."

The woman's eyes narrowed as she studied us. "I'm Delilah. He's a nice guy. I'd tell you if he was an ass."

Chase chuckled before turning away. Delilah was already serving someone else a drink. A moment later, she made her way over and paused beside me. "If you need any-thing, let me know. And I wasn't joking. Chase is a good guy."

I felt hot all over. "Okay, thank you."

"You take care," she said. Her eyes searched mine, and I sensed she knew I was struggling with something, but she was a stranger. Just as Chase was. And I wanted it to stay that way.

Chapter Two

CHASE

Hallie peered up at me, her stunning eyes blinking behind her glasses. "No last names," she announced.

My system felt electrified. My heart was drumming hard and fast in my chest as I stared down at her. "Okay." I heard myself saying.

I didn't know how I knew, but I knew this woman needed to forget something as much as I did. And maybe we could use each other to forget. The chemistry between us was enough to start a bonfire. Although I wasn't out searching for romance—unlike most of my friends lately who were falling in love at the speed of light—this woman gave me pause. Even though I liked to keep things casual, I wasn't an asshole.

"Just tonight," she added. "I don't live here."

I glanced down at her drink. "I've only had half of that. I'm not even buzzed," she clarified, somehow reading my mind.

"Okay," I repeated.

She slipped her hand into mine, her touch a little cool. I followed as she weaved her way through the bar. I caught the eye of my friend Ward as I passed by. His eyes dipped down to our hands. His gaze was unreadable when it lifted to mine again.

Moments later, we were standing outside what I presumed was her room on the third floor. For a second, I hesitated, doubts jostling in my mind. But then, she leaned up, slid her hand around the back of my neck, and brought her lips to mine, tugging me down just far enough to meet her. Her lips were plump and plush and warm. "Come on," she murmured, the words forming against my mouth.

I couldn't help it. I *needed* to taste her, so I deepened our kiss. When her tongue glided against mine, it felt as if threads of fire spun through my body, a tangle of heat and fierce need burning in the wake of sparks leaping.

I lifted my head, taking in her light-brown hair. It fell just above her shoulders in a swingy bob. Her eyes were a swirl of green and gold with flecks of brown and tilted up at the corners. She lifted her chin slightly as if she dared me to second-guess this.

Then the door opened, and she drew me inside. I forgot myself in her. In us.

When I woke the next morning, she was gone.

A tiny, square sticky note was left on the door.

Don't forget the rules: One night, no last names. It was everything I wanted. Thank you, Chase.

xo

Hallie

I lifted the note off the door, staring down at it before I folded it carefully and slipped it into my wallet for some reason.

I *had* wanted just one night, but it had been far more than I expected. Fuck me. We just clicked. I remembered Hallie's hazel eyes darkening. I remembered the feel of her clenching around me. I remembered falling asleep beside her and thinking maybe I could talk her into another night this morning. All I knew was her first name and that she was a photographer. I didn't even know where she lived. We'd traded very few details about each other. She knew I was Chase, I was from Willow Brook, and I was a firefighter. But that was it. I wanted to find her. But that was breaking the rules.

I took a shower in the room and made my way downstairs, stopping in the bar to see if Delilah happened to be around this early. She was. Her dark hair was pulled into a ponytail, and she glanced over at me with a crooked smile. "Good morning, Chase. Don't usually see you here in the morning."

A few guests had breakfast over in the buffet section that was set up in the mornings. Delilah was stocking the bar and tidying up.

"You usually work a late shift and then again in the morning?"

"Nah. I like the morning shift better. I was covering for someone last night. What's up?"

I eyed her, wondering whether to ask. Fuck it. "What are the chances you could get Hallie's last name for me?"

"Zero," Delilah said flatly.

"Come on," I pressed.

"No, that's totally not cool."

"But you vouched for me. You told her I was a nice guy," I insisted.

"Yeah, you are a nice guy, but if she didn't give you her last name and you try to get it, that's weird. I don't want to get fired for giving out customer information."

I sighed. "You're right."

She gave me a measured look and then leaned over. "If you meant as much to her as she did to you after last night, I'm sure she'll come back and find you. What does she know about you?"

"That I'm from Willow Brook and a fire-fighter, and my name is Chase."

"What do you know about her?"

"Her name is Hallie, she's some kind of a photographer, and she's not from Willow Brook. That's it."

"Hmm," Delilah said.

"You won't reconsider?"

"No, I won't. I don't even have access to the database for guests. I just cover the bar."

"All right," I grumbled. "See you around."

"You want some breakfast?"

"Nah, I'm gonna go to Firehouse Café."

She nodded in understanding. "We have coffee, but it's not that good."

I chuckled. "Thanks again."

"For what? I didn't even give you the info you wanted this morning."

"No, but you vouched for me last night."

"Because you *are* a good guy." Delilah winked and spun away.

As I left, I wondered if I could find Hallie or if it was better to leave last night exactly as it was.

Chapter Three

HALLIE

Three months later

"Um, what?"

My doctor studied me before nodding slowly. "You're pregnant."

"Why? How? Oh, my god!" I sputtered.

"Well, I presume you got pregnant the usual way. You've been attributing these symptoms to endometriosis, but that's not it."

"Oh, wow." I sat there in shock as I tried to absorb this news.

"I'm assuming you have a boyfriend then," Dr. Williams added.

"Uh, no. We used condoms."

She nodded. "Well, since we'd just re-moved your IUD the month before, you had a higher chance of getting pregnant." My IUD had expired, so she'd removed it. Since I'd planned to schedule surgery, I'd chosen not to get another one at the time.

"But, how did I get pregnant?" My brain felt thick, as if I was missing something.

"Because no birth control is 100 percent," she said matter-of-factly.

"Oh." I paused, trying to collect my thoughts. "But with endometriosis, my chances weren't that good."

She shrugged. "There *was* a chance."

"How far along am I?"

"Ballpark, three months."

I silently did the math in my brain. I'd met Chase—oh, my god!—almost exactly three months ago. I swallowed and took a shaky breath. "Okay, what do I do?"

"What do you mean?"

"Can I safely have a baby?"

"Just like birth control, I can't make guar-antees, but yes, you can safely have a baby."

"But you told me my chances of success-fully getting pregnant were very low."

"Low doesn't mean impossible. Did you think it was impossible?"

I sighed, swinging my legs where they

were dangling from the exam table. "Well, yeah, I did. I was about to look into the whole IVF thing because I wanted to do that before I lost the chance completely."

Dr. Williams sat down across from me on a stool. "You're pregnant. If you want to keep the baby, I think you should. Endometriosis is chronic, and we know you have a severe case. The last time you had surgery, it was stage four. Even though we've been doing things to manage it, you already have another cyst on one of your ovaries, and it's getting larger."

"Will that cause problems with my pregnancy?"

"We can deal with it."

I took a deep breath, still trying to scramble my thoughts together.

"Is the father someone you're friendly with? Will he support you in this process?" she asked gently.

"Well, uh, I don't know."

Her lips twitched. "I'm not here to lecture you on any of your choices. I asked because if you decide to keep this baby, you might want to talk to the father. It's been my experience, not as a therapist or a lawyer, but as a doctor who hears lots of stories, that things can get complicated when parents aren't kept in the loop about what's happening. It's your body and your choice. I'm 100 percent on your side with that. But communicating with him may be a way to head off any future complications."

I felt emotionally and mentally bombarded with issues I hadn't ever planned to contemplate. I swallowed. "Okay, what do I do?" I asked again.

She smiled softly. "For now, you start taking prenatal vitamins. We have samples here that you can leave with. Beyond that, let's schedule your next appointment. While you're pregnant, I'll need to see you regularly for monitoring and so on. It's six months out, but some of the surgical decisions we were waiting on could be handled immediately following delivery."

"You mean right after I have a baby?" I yelped.

She nodded, all cool and calm. "It's less traumatic for the body than another procedure. Many women get their tubes tied and even have a hysterectomy immediately after birth."

"Will the endometriosis come back?"

"You have a severe case, so that would be my assumption. On the upside, the recovery won't seem like a separate event."

"Really?"

"You'll be recovering from labor. What we would do surgically is less invasive than vaginal delivery or a C-section."

Everything she said was completely matter-of-fact. Meanwhile, my internal state was in emotional chaos. "Oh!" I started laughing. "That's hysterical."

She smiled. The intercom in her office sounded, indicating her next appointment had arrived.

"I have lots of questions," I said.

"I know you do. Let's make an appointment in two weeks. In the meantime, pick up the sample prenatal vitamins on the way out. Write down all your questions, so we can cover everything at your next appointment. In the meantime, congratulations," she said softly as she stood. "I know you wanted this possibility."

After Dr. Williams left, I sat on the table for a few more minutes, trying to absorb this insane information. I was pregnant. I felt like I should've known, except my reproductive system was so out of whack. I dealt with cramping, periodic bleeding, no periods, feeling sick, and intense pain so often that I had simply overlooked the symptoms, chalking them up to endometriosis. I *had* felt a fullness. However, I'd also had a seven-pound cervical cyst removed two years prior. So fullness was no big deal. That cyst had been the weight of a freaking baby.

As I got dressed, I contemplated my doctor's comments about discussing my choice with the father. There was *only* one person who could be the father. All I knew was his first name, his job, and the town he lived in forty-five minutes away.

Chapter Four

HALLIE

I stared up at the sign—Wildlands Lodge & Restaurant. It was daylight, and the place looked exactly as I'd remembered. With the exception that it was now spring, the snow was melting, and the ice was starting to break up on the lake behind the lodge.

It was late morning, and a mist was rising where the sun's rays angled across the water. An eagle screeched somewhere nearby, with a magpie chattering in return. My heart thudded unsteadily in my chest. I was so nervous, and I wasn't sure if I could find Chase.

This place was my best chance. The woman who'd worked at the bar that night knew who he was, so maybe she could point me in the right direction. I also knew he was a firefighter. But we hadn't discussed where he worked, though. In town or somewhere else?

I looked down at my belly. I was just starting to show at four months. Oddly, my pregnancy was the calmest my endometriosis had ever been. I was used to chronic pain and occasionally debilitating pain and cramps that led to vomiting because the pain was so intense. My morning sickness hadn't been that bad. Another clue that I had overlooked. I should've known. My doctor kept reminding me my symptoms of endometriosis could mimic pregnancy, including the bloating and the sense of fullness and discomfort.

I couldn't sit in my car forever, so I finally took a deep breath and climbed out, striding quickly through the back entrance. When I walked into the restaurant area, guests were eating at the buffet. The very buffet that I had taken a few muffins from and then left in a hurry, hoping I would get out of there before my one-night stand man woke up.

I looked over at the bar, and the nervous feeling in my belly spun faster when I saw Delilah there. She was stocking the shelves behind the bar and hadn't seen me yet. I walked across the empty bar area, stopping when I reached the polished counter.

I cleared my throat. "Excuse me?"

Delilah turned. She was striking with dark hair and dark eyes. She had a warmth to her but also a guardedness. "Yes?" She studied me, and I sensed she recognized me but couldn't quite place me.

"Uh, hi. Delilah, right?" I prompted.

Her dark brows rose as she nodded. "Yeah. I don't remember your name, but I probably served you here."

"Um, yeah, you did." My voice came out squeaky, and I cleared my throat again. "I'm hoping to find someone, and I think you might be able to help me."

She cocked her head to the side, and then her eyes widened. "That's how I recognize you. I vouched for Chase and told you he was a nice guy."

"You did. Um, I'm hoping you can tell me his last name."

"Why do you need to know his last name? Surely, he would've told you if he wanted you to know."

This was when I felt stupid and ridiculous. How in the hell did I end up in this situation?

I decided to go with blunt honesty.

"Look, it was a one-night stand. That's all we ever meant it to be. I don't have his number. I don't know his last name, but I really need to talk to him. It's important." Delilah studied me. "I know he's a firefighter," I added as if maybe that would be enough information for her to give me more.

"He is. I'm sure if you stopped by Willow Brook Fire & Rescue, they might be able to point you in the right direction," she finally said.

"Okay."

"On Main Street, you'll see Firehouse Café. Keep going past that, and it's on the right."

"Thank you. If I don't track him down, can you do me a favor and let him know you saw me here?" I fished a pen and a piece of paper out of my purse, writing down my full name. "Here's my phone number. I live in Anchorage. You can even give him my address." I added that and thrust the paper toward her.

She held my gaze for several long beats. "I'll pass on your message."

"Thank you," I said, biting back my sigh of relief.

"No problem. Take care, Hallie."

I swallowed. "I will."

"Okay, that wasn't so bad," I said to myself a few minutes later as I drove my car down Main Street.

I passed the café where I'd had coffee before, thinking I would stop there after I went to the fire station. I hoped I would find Chase, or at the least, discover a way to find him.

I pulled into the parking area in front of Willow Brook Fire & Rescue. My heart was pounding again. Oh, my god, I hardly knew Chase. That night had been memorable and the best sex I'd ever had. As intimate as we'd been, I didn't *know* him. I still couldn't get over the fact that I'd somehow gotten pregnant despite using condoms. But, but, but... things had gotten pretty hot and heavy before that condom made it on.

I didn't let myself wait in the car. If I did, I knew the anxiety spinning inside would intensify until I freaked myself right out. I walked briskly through the front entrance, hoping I somehow looked calm even though I felt as if I were teetering on the edge of a full-blown panic attack.

A woman with pretty brown curls and big brown eyes looked up from where she sat behind a circular desk in the reception area, smiling as she finished a call on her headset. I stopped in front of the desk, and she tapped a button after saying, "Thank you." Glancing up, she added, "Hi, can I help you?"

"Yes, um, I'm looking for Chase."

"Sure, he's here today. Give me a sec. I'll page him."

Wow. That was way easier than I thought. Now comes the hard part.

She tapped a button, saying, "Chase, someone's up front to see you."

I noticed the freckles scattered on her cheeks when she looked back up at me. She eyed me curiously, asking, "So who are you?"

"I'm Hallie, Hallie Thomas."

"I'm Maisie. Nice to meet you. How do you know Chase?"

I didn't feel like I could tell her we had a crazy hot one-night stand and didn't exchange last names or phone numbers, so I just said, "Um, he's a friend, sort of..." My words were trailing off when I heard footsteps approaching, and a door I hadn't even noticed before to the side of her desk swung open.

Chase, the man of multiple orgasms with dark hair, dark eyes to match, and a tall, delectable build, came striding through. He was looking at the floor and glanced up at the last moment. He almost stumbled when his eyes landed on me.

"Hallie?"

"Hey, hi."

"Ah, wow. I didn't expect to see you."

"I imagine not," I offered. "Do you have a few minutes to talk?"

He looked at me for several beats. I happened to glance to the side to see Maisie unabashedly looking between us, clearly curious and not the least worried we might notice.

"Uh, sure," Chase said slowly.

"Cade just left to go to Firehouse Café. You can use his office," Maisie offered helpfully.

Chase nodded and immediately opened the door, holding it as I walked by. A moment later, we were standing inside a square office with a desk and a small round table.

Chase's eyes searched my face. "I didn't expect to see you," he repeated.

I took a shaky breath, nodding. "Well, we didn't plan to see each other again."

"I can't say I'm not happy to see you. What's up?" he asked.

I was a rip the Band-Aid off kind of girl, so I just went for it. "I'm pregnant."

Chapter Five

CHASE

"I'm pregnant."

Hallie's words rang like a gong, reverberating through my brain. I stared at her, not realizing my mouth had dropped open until she added, "I'm surprised too."

Snapping my mouth shut, I stared at this woman I hadn't been able to forget. I'd resisted the urge to try to find her. Although Alaska was geographically large, it was small when it came to its residents. If I'd tried, I probably could have found her. But I had remembered Delilah's observation.

I'd figured it would be the hottest night of my life for the rest of my life, and I would always wonder what happened to Hallie.

"We used a condom," I stated the obvious.

"I know."

As the information slowly filtered through the shock into my rational brain, I gave my head a little shake. I glanced down at her belly when she smoothed her hand over it. She was just barely showing.

"I didn't know until a few weeks ago."

"How far along are you?"

"Four months."

I nodded, absorbing that detail. "What do you want to do?"

"I want to keep the baby," she whispered, her pretty hazel eyes searching mine.

My heart felt as if it gave a rounding kick inside my rib cage. My breath seized for a moment before I dipped my chin. "Okay."

"Is that okay with you?"

"It's your decision."

"I know, but what you think matters," she whispered.

I took a moment, almost as if testing the idea out in my brain. I'd always figured I'd eventually want kids. Did I want a child with this woman who I didn't really know? Other than that, we'd had the best sex of my life. In the end, those answers didn't really matter. What mattered was, "Yes."

Hallie must've been holding her breath because she let it out in a big sigh, her palm coming to her chest. "Thank god."

"Yeah?"

"Well, I didn't know how you might feel. I wasn't planning on this."

She took a deep breath. For a second, I thought she was going to fall when she wobbled on her feet. I stepped to her side swiftly, sliding one arm around her waist as I snagged a chair at the table nearby and pulled it close before easing her into it. "Are you okay?"

"Yes." She sank down with another sigh. "I am. I was kind of freaked out about trying to find you and didn't know if I could."

"How did you find me?"

"Well, I knew your name was Chase and that you lived in Willow Brook, and you're a firefighter. I started at Wildlands. Delilah wouldn't give me your last name, but she told me to come here."

"Mills," I said.

"What?"

"That's my last name, Mills."

"Oh. Mine is Thomas. Delilah has my name and phone number on a piece of paper. I asked her to give it to you, so if she does, that's why."

I felt my lips tugging into a smile. Hallie looked up at me, her gaze earnest.

"Good to know. Why don't you give me your number now? Since, well, since we're having a baby together. Are you sure I'm the father?" I belatedly thought to ask.

Hallie nodded quickly. "Absolutely, positively. I understand why you might not believe me, so we can do a paternity test if you want."

I shook my head. "I believe you."

Considering my own background, that was kind of amazing.

"Maybe we should do a test after the baby's born anyway," she commented.

"Why?"

"Because it'll just make it for sure for you. I don't know what will happen with us."

I shrugged. "All right, if you say so."

"It makes it clean, you know? Straightforward."

"Sure. I'm not an asshole, if you're wondering."

"I know you're not."

"Are you sure, though? We only had one night together," I offered bluntly.

Pink bloomed on her cheeks, and lust jolted me. Fuck me. *This* woman. All she had to do was blush, and it set my body on fire.

I slipped my phone out of my pocket. She fumbled in her purse and pulled her phone out. I entered her number as she recited it, smiling to myself as I added her last name.

"What?" she prompted.

"It's nice to know your last name."

I quickly sent her a text: *It's Chase Mills. You know? The no-last-names guy.*

She laughed softly, her eyes dipping down.

"I wanted to find you," I said, deciding to be honest.

Her eyes widened.

"That night was pretty amazing, and I couldn't forget you."

"How come you didn't?"

"Delilah pointed out if you'd wanted me to know your last name, you would've told me. I'd asked her if I could get your last name from the hotel. She had a point."

"I wanted to find you too, but I thought it might be weird. Then I found out I was pregnant."

"When do you see the doctor again?"

"In two weeks."

"Can I go with you?"

Hallie's brows rose.

"I'd like to be involved. It's really important."

She nodded slowly. "Okay, I'll text you the

appointment information and where it is. It's in Anchorage. Will that be okay?"

"I'll make it okay."

Chapter Six

HALLIE

I stared up at Chase, my heart hammering in my chest. I didn't know what I'd expected, but I supposed it wasn't this. I was startled that he wanted to come to a doctor's appointment with me.

A part of me wanted to backtrack, but that didn't feel right.

"It's in the morning. Is that okay?"

"Like I said, I'll make it okay. Morning is actually better for me."

"Um, okay." I sat there, not sure what to say next. What do you say to the hottest and only one-night stand of your life? In my mind, I'd tried to intellectualize it and tell myself I'd made him more handsome in my memories than he actually was. Yet having him here in front of me again, living and breathing—holy smokes. Chase Mills was a potent force—pure, raw masculinity with something I couldn't quite sort out. There was an intensity to him. Although I didn't have enough information to make an informed decision, I sensed he was a trustworthy man.

The fact that he'd wanted to look for me —which even I could admit, was a bit thrilling—but hadn't when Delilah had told him not to since I hadn't given him my last name or number only built onto the layer of trust I already felt for him.

"What do we do now?" I heard myself asking.

Chase sat down in the chair closest to me at this small round table. "I have no idea. I don't know what the rules are for this."

"For what?" I asked inanely.

"A woman I met once and had the hottest night of my life with showing up and telling me she's pregnant. I don't know what the rules are for that."

I burst out laughing. It was such a relief to finally find him and tell him because I didn't want to keep this a secret. His responding low chuckle sent my belly spinning in flips. I placed my hand over it reflexively.

His eyes dipped down and then lifted to mine again.

"How is it going?"

"What?" I asked.

"Your pregnancy."

"Okay, I guess. I only had a little bit of morning sickness. I know we used condoms," I added.

"We did," he affirmed.

"I, uh, have endometriosis. It's really kind of a surprise that I'm pregnant at all."

"So we've really beat the odds." His eyes widened.

"According to my doctor, yes. She pointed out that birth control is never 100 percent. But in my case, it's even more of a surprise because of the endometriosis."

"I don't know a lot about endometriosis. I just know it can cause problems." He shifted his shoulders, his gaze questioning.

I swallowed. "That's one way to put it. I'm supposed to have surgery, or I was." He nodded. "But I'm putting it off until after the baby now. Endometriosis is when uterine tissue grows outside of the uterus. It can grow all over your organs nearby and mess up your fertility. It's not that I'm infertile, but more that the endometriosis can interfere with things."

Chase studied me and nodded again, so I continued. "I also didn't pick up that I was pregnant a little earlier because, well, things have just been a mess for me for years. I always have weird symptoms and chronic pain and cramping. All of the things that come with pregnancy didn't set off any alarm bells because I rarely have my period either." I took a quick breath. "Oh god, I feel like I just unloaded a bunch of information on you, and you probably didn't need to know any of it."

He shrugged. "It's okay. You're just explaining. Is it going to affect your pregnancy?"

"Maybe? I don't know. I've had this doctor for years, so she knows everything that's going on, and she's on top of it. Now that I'm past the first trimester, she says things look healthy."

"Do you know if it's a boy or girl yet?" he asked.

I shook my head quickly. "I thought I'd wait to see if I could find you, and we could decide that together if you wanted to be part of this."

His eyes held mine, the brown darkening to espresso. My pulse kicked off, and I felt a little breathless. I broke away from his gaze, looking down at my hands. My fingers were laced together tightly, and I rubbed my thumb over a ring. When I dared to look up again, his eyes were waiting, steady and calm.

"Look... obviously, this is all news to me," he began.

I laughed a little, an edge of hysteria bubbling over. "Yeah, yeah, it is."

"I don't want to push too hard, but I do want to be involved. I understand if you don't want me at appointments and things, but—"

"It's okay," I said hesitantly. "I guess I didn't know if I would find you. I didn't want this to be a secret."

"We'll just have to figure it out," he said matter-of-factly. "So what happens at the next appointment?"

"It's a checkup, and they'll do an ultrasound."

"When do they check for the baby's gender if we want to know? Do you want to know?"

"I don't know. Sometimes. What about you?"

When Chase smiled, my belly felt all fluttery and tingly. "I don't know. I haven't really had time to think about it."

Just then, the door to the office swung open, and the man entering came to an abrupt stop. "Oh, I didn't know you were in here." The man with shaggy brown curls and piercing green eyes studied me for a moment before his gaze shifted to Chase.

"Sorry, Cade," Chase said as he stood. "This is Hallie."

I waved. "Hi."

"I'm Cade. Nice to meet you. How much longer do you need my office?" he asked, entirely unperturbed about our presence there.

Chase glanced down at me, and I shrugged.

"Why don't we go get some lunch?" he asked. "Mind if I leave?" He looked toward Cade.

"Go for it," Cade replied.

"How does that sound to you?" Chase asked.

I had been too nervous to eat earlier, so I was starving. "That sounds good."

When I stood, Chase stepped to my side, resting his hand on my lower back. The gesture felt protective, and I savored the feeling. Cade's sharp gaze bounced between us, and I sensed he had questions, but he simply smiled. "Nice to meet you, Hallie. Hope to see you again."

"You too, thanks."

We stopped in the hallway, and Chase

glanced down just as Cade closed the door behind us.

"Why don't I drive? I'll bring you back to your car afterward."

"Sure."

He led me down the back hallway into an open area with a kitchen to one side and a counter running along the wall. Some guys I presumed were firefighters lounged at the kitchen table. They all looked at me curiously as Chase waved. We passed into an area that had a large sectional and a television with some guys working out in a gym behind a glass wall beyond that. Firefighters appeared to be a handsome, very fit lot.

I eyed them to see if I had the same kind of reaction to any of these men that I did to Chase. I didn't. There was no fiery zing. It was just him. Just as we reached the back door, Maisie came walking out of a doorway and stopped. She held a stack of paper in her arms. "Hi," she said brightly as she glanced back and forth between us. "Everything okay?"

Chase chuckled. "Everything's good. We're gonna go grab lunch."

"Okay, will you bring me some coffee if you're going to Firehouse Café?"

"Sure thing," he replied. "Your usual?"

Maisie was nodding when someone else called out, "Coffee for me, please!"

Chase cast a grin over his shoulder. "Tell Maisie any orders, and she can text a list to me. I'll bring them back."

Maisie smiled at me again. "Nice to meet you, Hallie."

I waved, wondering if I would see any of these people again.

A few minutes later, Chase had led me into the café where I'd stopped for coffee the morning after our night together. "This is the old firehouse," he explained when he saw me eyeing the pole painted brightly with fireweed flowers in the middle of the café.

The cute and cheerful space had artwork on the walls and tables scattered throughout the room. The low hum of conversation reached us, and the scent of rich coffee and freshly baked goods filled the air.

When we reached the front of the line, the woman at the counter cast a beaming smile. "Hey, Chase."

"Hey, Janet. This is Hallie." He nudged his chin in my direction.

"Nice to meet you, Hallie. I'm Janet. I own this place. Good to have you here."

I managed to say something polite while my mind spun. I was still adjusting to the fact of my pregnancy, and now it felt surreal that I'd actually found Chase. I supposed it wouldn't have been all that hard, but with the situation, it felt monumental.

Chase said to Janet, "So Maisie is going to text me with coffee orders for the station." He lifted his phone to check the screen. "Nothing yet."

"Just forward me the text, and I'll get everything ready," Janet replied.

Chase chuckled as he slipped his phone back into his pocket. "You got it. What do you want?"

I looked up at the chalkboard. "Do you have any tea?" I asked Janet.

"Of course, I have tea. I make a mean cup of coffee too," she added.

"I'm not drinking coffee right now," I said quickly, realizing there were so many things I hadn't gone over in my head about finding Chase and telling him I was pregnant. Namely, were we talking about it with other people?

Janet simply reached under the counter and handed me a small chalkboard menu. "Teas are listed there."

"I'll take..." I scanned it and selected one.

A few minutes later, we were sitting down. I blurted out, "How are we handling this? Who are we telling? None of these people know me. I'm planning to tell my parents and my brother soon."

Chase leaned back in his chair, a smile slowly stretching across his face. "This is definitely on the list of things I hadn't thought about today. I'm sorry."

"I know, I know." My words rushed out. "This is a lot."

He shrugged easily. "It's okay. I can handle it."

We fell quiet, and I realized we hadn't talked much about ourselves during the single night we'd spent together.

"So all I know about you is you live here, you're a firefighter, and now I know your last name."

His eyes crinkled at the corners, and his gaze was warm. "And I know your name is Hallie Thomas, and you're a photographer. What kind of photography and where do you live?"

"Black and white. I do artsy stuff. I've been showcased in a few galleries, but I also pay a lot of bills by doing assignments for places. And I live in Anchorage."

"What do you mean?" he prompted.

"Location and feature photography, things like that. Alaska's good for it because of the touristy businesses. They want classy photos, and I make it happen."

"That makes sense. There's a gallery here in Willow Brook."

"I think I've heard of it."

"Midnight Sun Arts," he added.

"Oh, there's a location in Anchorage and my sister-in-law manages the one in Diamond Creek."

Chase nodded. "My friend Jasmine Ward does pottery. She sells it at Midnight Sun Arts in Anchorage and down in Diamond Creek. She must know your sister-in-law in Diamond Creek. Jasmine manages the one here," he explained.

"Oh, that's really cool! I'll have to swing by. I've seen her work in the Anchorage gallery."

Chase nodded and took a swallow of his coffee. "So you have a brother and parents then?"

I smiled, trying to ignore the nervousness spinning inside. "Yeah, my older brother lives in Diamond Creek. He's the police chief down there. My parents live in Anchorage."

"What about you?"

Chapter Seven

CHASE

Such a simple and entirely expected question. Considering I was talking to the woman I was going to have a child with, it was natural to ask about family.

I had family, and I loved them, but things felt complicated lately. I bit back a sigh and glossed over the situation. "I grew up right here in Willow Brook. My father lives here, and I have a sister. She's not in Willow Brook now, but she's planning to move back sometime. My mother passed away two years ago."

"Oh, I'm sorry," Hallie said quickly.

"Yeah, thanks." I ignored the sharp twist of my heart and the familiar hollow feeling in my stomach. To say my relationship with my mother had been complicated didn't accurately describe that shit show. I forged ahead. "Anyway, my dad's still here and doing well."

"That's nice. What does your father do?" she asked politely.

"He's an outdoor guide. He flies all over the state."

"That's cool. Alaska is definitely the place to do that."

"He loves it."

"It's kind of like your job since you must fly all over the state too."

She smiled, and I remembered I loved her smile. It was odd to see her again. I'd thought of her so many times in the past few months. I'd tried to convince myself the chemistry wouldn't snap and crackle like I'd recalled, and she wouldn't be as beautiful as I'd remembered. In a way, I suppose I'd tried to convince myself of that so I wouldn't keep thinking I'd let a chance pass me by.

I'd been wrong on both counts. She was more beautiful than I remembered with her glossy brown hair and chameleon-like hazel eyes. This sultry sweetness to her grabbed me like a fist around my heart. She set my nerves on fire. I belatedly realized I hadn't replied to her comment.

"I suppose, except I have to put out fires."

"There is that. Being a hotshot firefighter is kind of dangerous, isn't it?"

I shrugged. "Yes, obviously. But we know how to handle it."

"Being a firefighter suits you." She cocked her head to the side.

"You know that from one night?"

Her cheeks flushed pink. She pressed her lips together before pushing her glasses up on her nose. She'd been wearing glasses that night, and I loved them on her. "It's just a feeling really. Plus, I'm seeing you now, so it's not just one night."

Just then, Janet arrived with our sandwiches. I knew she was curious. She set the two plates down, looking at us. "I hope you love your sandwich," she said to Hallie.

"I'm sure I will."

"Let me know if you need anything else," Janet added.

I chuckled as she walked away. "What's funny?" Hallie asked.

"Janet. I love her dearly. I've known her since I was a kid. You can't grow up here without knowing Janet. I'm sure she's dying to know how I know you and what you're doing here. So what is the plan for how we talk about this?"

"You can tell whoever you want," Hallie

said with a little shrug. "I'm already showing. I'm wearing a loose jacket, so it's not that obvious to anyone who doesn't know me."

"What about us?"

"Us?" she chirped, her eyes going wide.

"Yes. I wanted to see you again," I said bluntly.

Hallie cleared her throat and took a swallow of her tea. "I don't know. I wasn't even sure how you'd feel about this. Chase, this is all—"

"A lot," I offered helpfully, repeating what she had said earlier.

She nodded earnestly. "Yes. I'm having a baby. You're the father. We hardly know each other."

"I know. That one night was really incredible, but I get it. We'll take it one step at a time." When she nodded and took a bite of her sandwich, I finally asked the questions that had been tumbling in my mind every time I thought about her. "What was that night about? Why did you say no last names, no phone numbers?"

She finished chewing and shrugged. "I've never had a one-night stand except for you. That was the day I'd had a talk with my doctor, the one who's monitoring my pregnancy. I was planning to schedule a hysterectomy because of the chronic problems with my endometriosis."

"Seriously?"

She nodded. "I've already had two surgeries to remove ovarian cysts due to endometriosis. Both times, they had to clean up a bunch of other tissue. I have chronic pain and damaged fallopian tubes. I'd decided that was the best option because it didn't look like I would ever get pregnant. Why keep going through so much pain? It's not like I was all about getting married and settling down, but I wanted the idea. I wanted the option of having kids, and it was a hit to make that decision. I just wanted to forget all my feelings. I saw you and decided one night was perfect."

"I appreciate your honesty," I finally said as I tried to wrap my brain around all that information. "It's kind of a miracle that you got pregnant," I added after a few bites of my sandwich.

She laughed softly. "Yeah, the odds were slim."

We ate quietly, and my mind spun. I was going to be a father, assuming everything went well for the next five months. Holy fucking shit.

We finished eating and drove back to the

station. I pulled into the front, asking, "That your car?" I gestured to the single car in the front parking lot.

Hallie nodded. I parked beside her and glanced over. I moved without thinking, leaning across the console. I palmed her cheek, peering into her eyes. I recalled how they darkened as she came when I was buried deep inside her. Since I wasn't thinking, I wasn't sure what I expected, but she didn't draw away.

We stared at each other quietly for several beats. I dipped my head, brushing my lips over hers. I didn't intend for this kiss to even happen, but before I knew it, it went from a dusting kiss to me fitting my mouth over hers. I slid my hand into her hair, sweeping my tongue in to glide against hers. She tasted just like I remembered—a little sweet. She sighed and kissed me back with abandon.

I practically pulled her across the console before my elbow hit the horn, and the sound snapped through the moment. We broke apart, both of us gulping in air. When I looked back over at Hallie, her eyes were wide, and then she burst out laughing.

"What?" I asked, my lips curling into a smile.

"You are too much."

"What do you mean?"

"I forget everything when you kiss me."

Since she was being honest, I decided to offer the same. "Well, you do the same thing to me."

She took a deep breath, pressing her palm to her chest.

"When can I see you again?" I asked.

"My doctor's appointment is in two weeks."

"Can I see you before that?" I surprised myself with that question, but we had a lot of territory to cover. I also desperately wanted to see her before then.

"Okaaa-y," she replied slowly.

"I'll drive to Anchorage, or you can come here. Whatever you prefer."

Her eyes searched mine before she nodded slowly. "Okay. Next weekend."

"I'll text you, and we can decide where to meet."

Chapter Eight

CHASE

The following day, my phone rang. I glanced down to where it sat on the counter in my kitchen. I was sitting on a stool, lingering over a cup of coffee. It was my sister calling. Again.

I answered, "Hey, Tiffany."

"Hey! I called you the other day, and you didn't call me back," she said.

"I know. I meant to. I've just been busy."

"That's what you always say. Are you okay?"

"Tiff, I'm fine. It's fine."

My sister charged right at any problem or person she worried about. Of late, that was me.

"Chase, you can't change the past. Dad

and I are fine with it, and I want you to be at peace."

"With what?"

"Mom's dead, and she lied."

"Tiff, I know you want to fix this. You want to fix everything. I just..." I paused, scrubbing a hand in my hair. "Look, the whole situation sucks. That's all."

Roughly a year ago, we'd collectively learned that my mother had lied about who my father was. The man who'd been the only father I'd known and the father of my heart was not my biological father. My mother had never told any of us before she passed away. We'd only found out because my sister had us do DNA tests out of curiosity to find out if we had more family out there. At first, all I'd learned was Tiffany and I didn't have the same father. I felt like my feet had been kicked out from under me. Mere weeks later, I received a message online from one of my half-siblings. I'd never know why my mother lied, and to make matters messier, I hadn't had a good relationship with her for most of my life.

She'd been *a lot* to deal with. My dad and I had always been tight, and we still were. Ever since this little bomb had landed in our lives, he had assured me every which way that he loved me as his son and always would. My bio dad had died before I'd even known he existed.

Lately, Tiff had been trying to get me to have a relationship with my other half siblings. I had seriously mixed feelings about it. The whole thing was a fucking mess. I had seven half siblings in Fireweed Harbor, a small town in Southeast Alaska. I'd never even visited there. Apparently, my mother had worked a summer job there and gotten pregnant just before she married my dad.

"Tiff, please let me figure this out at my own speed."

My sister's sigh filtered through the phone line. "All right. I'm sorry."

"I know you want to fix it. You've connected with them, and they sound great, but I just need a little bit more time."

"I know, I know. Can you promise not to blow off my calls? That's what gets me worried."

"I promise. I really was busy." I was always busy with life, but I knew I was grabbing onto an easy excuse. "You coming home anytime soon?"

"Yeah, I'll be there in a few weeks."

"Good. What else are you calling for?"

"Just to see how you're doing."

"Well, I've got news, and it's pretty big."

"What's that?"

"I'm going to be a dad."

"Excuse me? What?!" Tiff exclaimed.

"Yep. I'm as shocked as you."

"When did you find out?"

"Yesterday."

"Why didn't you call me right away?" I could practically hear her choking up. My sister was emotional and a total sweetheart.

"I promise I was gonna call. I was just adjusting to the news before I talked to anyone."

"That's you," she said softly. "So, um, I didn't even know you were seeing anyone."

"Well, uh, we weren't dating. I want you to know straight up we used birth control. This is a shock for her too. She wants to have the baby."

"And she wants you involved?"

"Well, she came and told me, Tiff."

"Well, but—"

"Don't go worrying that she's some kind of flake. She's not. Her name is Hallie Thomas, and she's a nice person. Her brother's the police chief in Diamond Creek. I'm pretty sure I don't have to worry about her background."

"I'm really glad she told you, Chase."

"Yeah, me too." While my brain was still wobbly with the enormity of the news, I was relieved Hallie hadn't kept this from me.

"When is the baby due?"

"In five months."

"Wow. Oh, my god. I'm so excited!" Tiff squealed. "Have you told Dad?"

"I'm having dinner with him soon, so I'm planning to tell him then. I'd rather tell him in person."

"Oh, Chase, you know if—"

"Tiff," I warned. "Please let me take this one step at a time. I'm not ready to talk to my new family about the baby on the way that I just found out about yesterday. They've invited me out to meet them, and I'll go when I'm ready."

"I know. It's just, your baby will be their relative."

"I know."

"All right. I'll back off," she said, her tone softening.

"No, you won't," I replied with a wry chuckle. "But I love you anyway."

My sister laughed. She had a giant heart, and she was kind to everyone.

"Can I meet Hallie?"

"I have to sort things out with us. And, yes, you will meet her, but I'm not going to force you on her immediately. I've only seen her twice."

"When are you going to see her again?"

"I'm going to meet her in Anchorage next weekend. She's already said I can come to her doctor's appointments."

"Oh, well, that's a good sign."

"That's what I thought."

"If and when you decide to reach out to your brother, please let me know."

"As if you wouldn't know before I even did," I teased lightly.

Tiff let out a sigh. Although she might be pushy about family in general, she didn't defend our mom because she had her own crosses to bear on that.

"Love you," she said. "Please keep me in the loop."

"Love you too. You're totally in the loop."

She laughed again, and we ended the call. Because she couldn't help herself, she texted me right after we hung up. *You can ask Archer about Rhys Cannon. He'll tell you all about him.*

Archer Cannon was a friend I'd gone to elementary school with. He'd moved away and come back this year. Turns out, Archer was actually my cousin through this whole convoluted situation. Rhys was his cousin and my oldest half brother from the family I hadn't known I had. Small fucking world.

Me: *Tiff, love you. I'll talk to Archer about this when I'm up for it.*

She sent me three hearts and hug emoticons in return.

Aside from finding out my father wasn't my bio father, I never knew my bio dad, and by all accounts, he'd been a decent guy. Now, he was dead. My mother had sliced him out of my life. I was profoundly grateful for the father of my heart, but I kept wondering what I'd missed.

To make matters even more complicated, this newly discovered family was seriously wealthy. An attorney had been in touch about ensuring I was included in the family business. I had mixed feelings about that because I didn't want it to seem like I wanted the money. For fuck's sake, I didn't need money. My life was perfectly fine just as it was.

That evening, I decided to text Hallie.

Me: *Hey, how's it going?*

She replied quickly.

Hallie: *Good. How are you?*

Me: *Pretty good.*

Hallie: *Are you going to start texting me every day?*

Me: *I just might. Is that a problem?*

Hallie: *No, it's not. Maybe we can get to know each other this way. Tell me your three favorite things to eat.*

Me: *Macaroni and cheese. Fresh king salmon cooked with butter and lemon. This tater tot casserole my dad made when I was a kid. Unhealthy and delicious. What about you?*

Hallie: *Ditto on the mac and cheese. My second would be fresh halibut. Love it. My third is this gooey scallop potato casserole that my mom makes. It's really good and loaded with cheese. Now, I want to try your tater tot casserole.*

Me: *I can make it for you.*

Hallie: *You can?*

Me: *Sure, my dad taught me to cook, and this recipe was a staple in our house. If you'll let me, I'll make it for you sometime.*

Hallie: *Deal. Let's do this every day.*

Me: *Do what every day?*

Hallie: *Three things.*

Me: *Okay. So I'll see you at your place, or should we meet somewhere?*

Hallie: *Let's start at my place.*

Me: *You got it.*

Hallie: *Good night, Chase.*

Me: *Good night, Hallie.*

After we stopped texting, I couldn't stop thinking about her. I'd had the hottest night of my life with Hallie, and now she was pregnant. Something was almost innocent about trying to get to know her like this. I couldn't wait to see her again. I was chafing to press for more sooner. Yet we had to get this right. There was a baby involved.

Chapter Nine

HALLIE

Lifting my phone, I scanned the screen, double-checking the grocery list I'd texted to myself. My eyes scanned to the text from Chase below it. I couldn't help but smile to myself again. I'd read this silly text more times than I could count all because of how it ended. *I can't wait to see you.*

I couldn't wait to see Chase. It had been barely a week since I'd seen him. I already felt like I was showing more. I looked down at my belly, smoothing my hand over it.

I was nervous, more nervous than I wanted to be. I kept telling myself it wasn't like this was the first time I was going to see Chase. I needed to get used to the idea of him being a part of my life.

My cheeks got hot all over. Every time I thought of him, vivid memories of the night we spent together came rushing back. I'd felt vulnerable and raw with him in a way I'd never felt with anyone. At the time, I told myself it was because it was a one-night stand and we were never going to see each other again. I'd let my guard down more. So much for one night.

If my pregnancy was healthy and I had this baby, Chase would be a part of my life for years and years to come.

I kept telling myself not to want anything from him, not to expect anything, but it was hard.

"Excuse me?" a voice said.

I glanced over my shoulder quickly to see a woman behind me. I was blocking part of the cheese section at the grocery store. "Oh, I'm sorry." I hurried out of the way.

Chase and I had kept up with our three things a day, which was turning out to be a low pressure way to get to know someone. I felt like this was all happening backward. We'd had hot sex, we were having a baby, and now we were getting to know each other. Funnily enough, I kind of liked it.

I returned home and put away the groceries. One more night until I saw Chase, and

I was seriously impatient. I was sitting on my couch, distractedly watching television when my phone rang. I glanced down to see my sister-in-law's name flash on the screen.

I adored Risa and considered her one of my closest friends, which was a gift because I was close to my brother, and it would have been awful if I hadn't liked his wife. I'd told them about my pregnancy just last week. I thought Darren was still adjusting. Sliding my thumb across the screen, I lifted the phone to my ear.

"Hey, how's it going?" I asked.

"Fine. How are you feeling?" Risa replied.

"Good. How's Darren? Or how is he adjusting to my news?"

Risa's throaty chuckle filtered through the phone line. "He wants to know how it's going with the father, and he offered to help."

"I found him, and it went well."

"Soooo?"

"So what?" I returned.

She let out a huff. "What is he like, and what is his last name? You know Darren's going to look him up."

"I know, and that's weird. His name is Chase Mills, and he lives in Willow Brook. He's a firefighter for one of the hotshot crews there. He grew up there. He has a sister, and his father is still alive, and they're close. I already told you that the bartender vouched for him."

"Right, but who is the bartender?"

"She's very nice. Her name is Delilah. She works at Wildlands."

"Oh, I think I've been there once. I'm going to ask Jasmine about him."

"Huh?"

"Jasmine Ward. She runs the gallery there."

"Oh, that's right! Chase mentioned he knows her."

"I'm sure she knows all about him because Levi Phillips is her brother. He's a hotshot firefighter, and she's married to Donovan, who's also a hotshot firefighter," Risa added.

"Oh, my god. The world is too small," I muttered. "It doesn't feel right to have you nosing around about him."

"You know you want me to," Risa teased. "Be honest with me."

I burst out laughing. "Okay, fine. Maybe a little info would be good."

"I might as well get as much information as I can. This man is the father of your baby."

"Does Darren think I'm irresponsible?"

"Whoa. You're an adult. If you want to

have a no-strings one-night stand at any time, that is completely within your rights."

"Well, I know that, but he is my older brother, so he might have an opinion."

"Yeah, whatever. I don't think he cares. He just wants to make sure the guy is decent and going to be there for you financially."

"I think he will be."

"I bet he has good health insurance since he's a firefighter. Maybe you should get married."

"Oh, my god," I sputtered. "You're getting ahead of yourself."

"You're having a baby. That's more serious than getting married," she replied, her tone pragmatic.

I sighed. "I know. I hope it's okay. He seems nice, and we'll be okay. Is Darren around?"

"Actually, he's covering the evening shift because one of the cops is on vacation this week. I thought it was the perfect time to call and get the scoop. I'll follow up and give him all the details so he's prepared when you talk to him."

"Poor Chase, he has no idea what dealing with my nosy police chief brother might be like."

"He's not stupid. I'm sure he knows your

family is going to look out for you. I'll do my homework on your behalf and talk to Jasmine and have her scout out all the information."

I shook my head even though she couldn't see me, laughing softly. "Wow. Well, I guess this is a bonus then."

"Totally is. When did you say you were seeing him next?"

"He's coming to Anchorage tomorrow, and he'd like to come back and attend my doctor's appointments with me."

"Wow, that's serious."

"I don't know. Is it good or bad?"

"Well, he wants to be involved. I think that's good."

"I hope so. I just hope he doesn't turn out to be a jerk."

"Did you think he was a jerk the night you met him?"

"No, but it was just one night."

"Here's the question I have that I don't expect you to answer for Darren: Was it good?"

I burst out laughing, my cheeks flashing with heat. "Uh, yes. It was the best night I ever had."

"Oh my," Risa said with a low whistle.

Meanwhile, I was hot all over. Feeling like I needed to shake the heat off my body, I stood from the couch and paced in a little circle around the coffee table.

"All right. Call me after you see him again. I want to hear about it. Are you going to let him stay the night?"

"I don't know. Oh, god, I don't know how to do this. I feel like we did it all backward."

"All you can do is deal with what's happened. That's it."

I took a breath. "Okay, you're right. That's all I can do."

Chapter Ten

HALLIE

Staring at myself in the mirror, I ran my fingers through my hair. I sighed as I studied my reflection. I had plain light-brown hair with a subtle sheen to it. I was doing that ridiculous thing where I tried to make it look styled without looking like I put any effort into it. I rolled my eyes. I turned my attention to my glasses, contemplating if I should stick with the blue frames or change them. I decided to stay with the blue frames.

I buttoned one of the buttons on my shirt and then unbuttoned it again. Wearing a silky blouse over a fitted tank top was a typical outfit for me because it was comfortable while still being sort of attractive. I couldn't decide how high up I should button my blouse. All the way up didn't make sense, but—

The doorbell rang. "Fuck," I squeaked.

With no more time to obsess over my appearance, I hurried down the hall. I had a small apartment in downtown Anchorage. The main room was a big rectangle with an angled ceiling and windows with a view of Cook Inlet. The kitchen was set to the back, and a short hallway to the side led to my bedroom and a bathroom with laundry.

Stopping in the living room in front of the door, I realized at the last second that my feet were still bare. My painted purple toenails looked up at me.

I took a breath and smoothed my hands over my jeans. I was actually sweating. I was usually cold, but pregnancy made me hot. On the heels of another breath, I opened the door.

"Hi," I squeaked.

Chase's lips kicked up into a smile, and my belly went wild, spinning with butterflies and sending tingles all over. "Hey, Hallie," he said, his voice low.

He sounded calm, the opposite of how I felt. My pulse was galloping. I cleared my throat, trying to take another breath, but not getting much air. I stood there, frozen in place.

"Can I come in?" he asked.

His eyes dipped down to my bare feet, and my cheeks got even hotter when he lifted his gaze to meet mine again. "I haven't put my shoes on yet," I explained pointlessly. "Obviously, come on in."

I laughed to myself, the silly moment breaking through my anxiety. I stepped back, and he walked in. I watched his gaze scan the space. "Nice apartment."

I shrugged as I closed the door. "It's just me, so I don't need much space."

"It feels like you have plenty with the high ceiling."

He walked to the windows, sliding his hands in his pockets as he did. I took the moment to surreptitiously look him over. He was wearing a pair of black jeans, faded and comfortably molded to his muscled thighs. The sun was starting to lower in the sky, offering a gorgeous view of Cook Inlet with the colors shimmering on the water.

"Beautiful," he commented.

He wore a long-sleeved Henley atop his jeans. I absorbed the way his shoulders filled it out. Chase was built, but then it wasn't as if I didn't know that. I'd felt his muscled back under my palms when I clutched him against me as he filled me and sent me flying.

I swallowed, my cheeks flashing with heat again when he turned around. I was still just standing there by the doorway, stuck in place. I shook my head, saying, "Let me get my socks."

I hurried down the short hallway into my bedroom, sliding on a pair of lightweight socks before returning to the living room and crossing to where he politely waited by the windows. I glanced up. "How was the drive?"

"It's a pretty drive from Willow Brook to Anchorage and really not that far."

"I suppose it isn't. I just haven't been to Willow Brook much."

"Had you ever been there before we met?"

I nodded. "Once or twice. I usually go to Diamond Creek if I need a getaway from Anchorage."

"Oh, yeah. You mentioned your brother lives in Diamond Creek, right?"

I nodded. "He moved there a few years ago."

"It's beautiful down there. I've been to the ski lodge."

"Oh yeah, that's a nice place. I'm not that

great at skiing, though. I stick to the bunny slopes."

Chase's teeth flashed with his grin. "I prefer the backcountry trails. We should go sometime."

My stomach growled, and I slapped my hand over my belly.

"Hungry?" he teased.

"All the time," I said.

"Let's eat then. Are we eating in or out?"

"Let's go out."

"Just tell me where to go."

"I thought we could go to the brewery and burger place nearby. They have great food, and we can walk."

"Ah, I've gotten beer from here although I've never eaten there. How's the food?"

"Excellent. They have a good variety from basic pub stuff to fancier things. Since I didn't know what you liked, I figured that would give us options."

"I am a fan of options," he replied with a grin.

As we walked out of my building, he rested his hand on my lower back, gesturing me through the door. I didn't want his touch to leave.

He stopped on the sidewalk, glancing down. "How are you?"

I looked up, puzzled. "Good," I said slowly.

"How are you with this? I should say."

My heart started to beat faster, my body's response tangling within the fact that it couldn't forget that night with him. It didn't help that he was so damned sexy. Oh. My. God. Just looking up into his dark eyes sent heat rushing through me.

"By this, you mean having dinner?"

"This meaning having dinner, meaning we had a hot night, and now you're having a baby."

"Um, it's a lot, but I think it's good." My belly spun in flips.

His eyes searched mine. "I'm going to kiss you," he said, his voice low and deliberate.

I felt breathless as I nodded. Then his hand was sliding into my hair. It felt as if he was going slow, almost as if to give me a chance to say no. I couldn't, and I didn't want to. I knew what Chase's kisses were like, and they were toe-curling and meltingly good.

The second his lips brushed over mine, my entire body sizzled with anticipation. I felt the press of his fingers against the back of my scalp and his thumb brushing along the side of my neck. I let out something like a gasp just before he fit his mouth over mine, his tongue sweeping in. Once again, I forgot everything, just as I had the night we made a baby, the very baby I was now carrying.

By the time he broke away, I was breathless and feeling hot, needy, and restless. I had one arm clutched around his waist and the other clinging to his shoulder as I stared up at him. He held me fast against him.

His fingers loosened in my hair, and his hand slid down, his thumb brushing along the side of my jaw. "Fuck, Hallie," he murmured.

"What?" I rasped.

"You make me crazy."

"I know the feeling," I managed to tease in return. I laughed a little, almost in shock, almost in awe, and tied up with a need that only he could unravel.

Chapter Eleven

CHASE

Hallie cleared her throat and looked over at me before pushing her glasses up on her nose. I loved her glasses. She was beautiful in a quiet way, the kind of woman who didn't draw too much attention.

All I had to do was look into her eyes, the swirl of green and gold, let my eyes trail over the freckles dusting her cheeks and the way her hair caught glimmers of light, and my heart pounded harder. Her lips were a little fuller on the bottom and a hint of lopsided. I loved how whenever she smiled, it started on one corner and spread to the next with a subtle dimple. So much of her was subtle. The more time I spent with her, the more I noticed new details. Yet I couldn't forget our night together, which had been anything but subtle. That night with her had been like trying to hold a living flame in my arms.

There was a boldness to her that I sensed she rarely showed. "What did you want that night?" I surprised myself by asking.

She blinked, and that very smile spread from one corner to the other. My cells tightened in anticipation—not for her answer, although I *did* want to know the answer—but for what might happen, hopefully sometime in our future.

"Like I told you, it's a fluke that I got pregnant. Not impossible."

"Clearly not," I interjected dryly.

"I think I told you this, but I had just left an appointment with my doctor. I was supposed to schedule surgery. That same day, an ex who I'm friends with—" She paused, adding, "He's married."

"Does that matter?" I prompted.

"No. We've been best friends since middle school. We tried to date. We joke that I was the one who helped him figure out he preferred men."

"How is that?"

"Well, we were friends. He figured if he

would fall for anybody, it would be me. But nothing. We tried kissing once." She rolled her eyes. "We couldn't even go through it. For me, it felt like I was about to kiss my brother. Anyway, he and his husband are having a baby via surrogate, and she's already pregnant."

"That's great, right?"

"Yes, of course. It *is* great. I know this might sound selfish and weird, but it was hard to realize I didn't think I could have a baby and wonder why it was so easy for someone else. Or that's what I thought." She paused, her lips pressing together as she shook her head. "It just feels really selfish. But anyway, I heard that news within a day of learning that I probably needed to make this decision."

"But you got pregnant," I couldn't help but interject.

"Yeah, but I didn't know that might happen, and the chances were incredibly slim. Even this pregnancy won't change the state of my reproductive organs. It's a mess in there."

"Really? I admit I don't understand all of it."

She nodded. "I've already had surgery

twice. I have stage four endometriosis. To make a long story short, I was in a weird mood, and I was feeling reckless. I just decided I was going to do something crazy."

"Having a one-night stand with me is crazy?" I prompted lightly.

Pink bloomed on her cheeks. She smiled slightly again, fiddling with a bracelet on her wrist. "For me, yes. Not that you're crazy, but just I'm not usually that reckless. Look where it got me. We were careful. I've definitely learned nothing is 100 percent."

"So I recall from sex ed in high school," I quipped with a somber nod and a wink.

Hallie burst out laughing when a server arrived to take our order.

"What can I get you two to drink?" the server asked.

"No, thanks. Just water for me," Hallie said.

"I'll stick with water too." Normally, I would get a beer, but Hallie couldn't drink.

The server told us he'd be back with those and left the specials menu with us. As soon as he was out of earshot, she looked over at me. "You can have a beer, you know."

"I know. Solidarity, you know?"

"Chase, you hardly know me."

"Hmm, I might argue the point on that," I teased.

Her blush deepened, and she rolled her eyes.

We moved on to lighter topics. Among other things, she offered to send me a link to her website so I could see her photography. She shared she'd gotten a few lucky breaks.

"You have to be good enough to take advantage of a lucky break, though," I commented.

The moment I said that, my heart twisted a little. That was something my dad said all the time. He would always be my dad in every way that mattered, but it still stung that I hadn't known until recently that he wasn't, biologically speaking, my father. Now was not the time to dwell on that.

"True, but you know what I mean?" she insisted.

"I get it. I do."

"So how'd you become a firefighter?"

"I love doing stuff outdoors, simple as that. I did some volunteer work at the fire station in high school. I loved it, so I got a job there cleaning the place when I was younger. I kept doing that during summers while I was in college. After that, I got trained and took a job as a hotshot fire-fighter. I freaking love it."

"I bet it's thrilling," she offered.

I smiled over at her. "Thrilling is the way to put it. Some might say risky."

"It's hard for something to be thrilling if it's not risky," she said matter-of-factly.

"True."

"How often do you travel during the winter?"

"Not as much, unless we're called out of state, which we are on occasion. Three hot-shot crews, plus the town crew, are based in Willow Brook, and we rotate the calls in Alaska. Unfortunately, Alaska is a hot spot, no pun intended, for fires in the wilderness."

She nodded. "So you stay busy then?"

"Yeah, usually we travel for three-week stints. You can only stay out for so long without needing a break physically." I paused, considering something. "Are you worried I won't be around much for the baby?"

She quickly shook her head. "This is Alaska, Chase. Lots of people travel for work here. It's not that unusual."

A tension I hadn't even noticed spun inside. I'd only had a short time to adjust to the fact that I was going to be a fa-ther. Since learning the news, I hadn't dwelled much on my job, so I was profoundly relieved to discover Hallie was practical.

She carried a sweetness, a softness undergirded by simple practicality.

"I'm glad you found me that night."

She stared at me for a long moment before cocking her head to the side. "Are you really?"

I nodded slowly but definitively. "Yes, I told you I wanted to find you after that night. But we had an agreement, and it didn't involve me looking for you."

"Yeah, but I'm pregnant. I don't think that was part of our plans."

I shrugged, adding quickly, "I'm not making light of it, but lots of things happen in life that aren't planned. It was a really good night. Unforgettable."

We stared at each other, and I could feel the electricity humming in the air, snapping and crackling.

Hallie took a quick breath and nodded.

"What if you didn't find me?" I had wondered about that a few times.

"I don't know. I would've asked my brother to track you down."

"The police chief?"

She nodded. "Lots of children don't know

both of their parents, but I felt like it was my responsibility to try to find you."

I thought about my sister's comments about my half siblings who wanted to get to know me.

"Are you really comfortable having me come to your doctor's appointment?"

She laughed softly. "Doctor's appointments are kind of boring and personal."

"I don't have to come in the room."

"It's fine. I mean..." Her cheeks tinged with pink. "I don't—" she began and then paused. "I don't know how to do this."

"We're going to have to figure it out on the fly. We don't really have any choice."

"No, I suppose not."

We fell quiet when the server arrived to bring our check. After he left, Hallie looked up.

"Thank you," she said softly.

"For what?" I slipped my credit card out.

She reached for her purse. "I'll pay half."

"I'll get it tonight. You can get it next time if you insist."

"Okay."

"But what are you thanking me for?"

"You could have been mad when I came to find you and told you what happened. You might not want to have a baby, but you're being a really good sport about it."

"Look, I'm mature enough to know birth control isn't a guarantee. I also believe in being accountable. That's not the only reason I'm trying to be there for you, though. I'm really grateful you found me."

Chapter Twelve

CHASE

I tried to tell myself I needed to take things slow with Hallie, but my body wasn't having it. The entire time I sat through dinner with her, I felt tied up in knots. Need thrummed through me, making me restless.

My thoughts were hazed by the time we left. Moments later, we were standing outside the door to her apartment. She peered up at me, her eyes searching mine. "Would you like to come in?"

Hell. Fucking. Yes, I thought. In action, I simply nodded, and we walked into her apartment. She glanced around, commenting, "I wish I could have a pet here."

She turned to face me. "I have a dog."

"You do?"

At my nod, her eyes lit up. "Jasper. He's good company."

She slipped out of her jacket and hung it up on the coat rack by the door, and I followed suit. Moments later, we were sitting on her small couch, which was the kind that pulled you right into its comfort with plenty of cushions.

Hallie curled her knees up, tucking her feet under her hips and asking, "What happens to your dog when you go out in the backcountry?"

"My dad takes care of him."

My mind suddenly conjured the image of Hallie at my house, *our* house, and my dog Jasper there with her and our baby. Fuck. I was getting *way* ahead of myself here.

"So do you live in town in Willow Brook?" she asked, oblivious to my domestic train of thought.

"A few minutes outside of town. I'm staying in a small house on some property I bought a few years back. I'm building a bigger place, but it's not done yet."

"Oh, that's awesome. When will it be done?"

I let out a sigh. "When I have enough time to finish it."

Hallie smiled. "There's never enough time."

"Never."

We looked at each other quietly, and it felt as if electricity was sparking in the air around us. The couch was small. It didn't take much for me to lean a little closer and dip my head. Palming her cheek, I murmured, "I want to kiss you."

"Okay," she whispered.

I waited for a beat, and I saw a flash of the fiery and bold woman I'd spent that one night with.

She pressed her palm lightly on my chest before sliding it up around my neck and tugging me down. One blazing second burned to the next as we kissed while sensations bombarded me—the feel of her lips warm and soft under mine, the glide of her teasing tongue, the sweet hitch of her breath in her throat, and the soft press of her curves against me when she shimmied closer. She felt both familiar and new. Even though that night was seared into my cellular memory, it was just one night. It almost felt like a mirage because of the boundaries we placed around it.

Our mouths broke apart, and we held fast to each other. I stared into the swirl of her eyes, trying to catch my breath, trying to slow the rush of need coursing through me. I took a steadying breath, and Hallie followed suit.

After a moment she asked, "What do you want, Chase?"

"You," I said bluntly.

I closed my eyes and took another breath, scrambling for control inside. When I opened them again, her lashes lifted to meet my gaze. "I told myself I wasn't going to rush this."

"We skipped a lot of steps," she whispered.

"That's one way to put it," I offered dryly.

"What if—" She paused, shaking her head quickly.

"What if, what?" I pressed.

"I don't know the best way to do this, but I know the only thing we can do is be honest. Obviously, we have chemistry."

A wry laugh rustled in my throat. "That's one way to put it," I repeated.

"But we're having a baby together. What if things get weird?" She paused. "I know I'm the one who insisted on no last names, no phone numbers, and just one night, but I don't want to have a casual relationship and have a baby together. That's confusing. I'm not saying you have to marry me and declare your undying forever love."

"I don't want a casual relationship either."

"How do you know?"

I shrugged. "I don't. I just know we had that one night, and I couldn't forget you. Even if it's startling that you're pregnant and we're doing this together, I wanted to see you again. And it wasn't just because I wanted only another night." Her lips quirked at the corners. "I liked you that night, and now I like you more."

She held up a hand. "We had one night together." Her thumb rose. "And then I came to tell you I was pregnant." She lifted her index finger. "Now we've had dinner together." She was holding three fingers up. "How do you know you want it to be something more? That doesn't seem like much of a foundation."

"I know, I know. I'm not crazy. I'm not going to try to pretend I know this will be easy. But I like you, and my gut tells me we should see where this goes. It's not going to be any easier to figure it out later. You're having a baby. If it seems like it's not going to work out, maybe it's better if we figure that out before the baby comes along, and we can find our way into a friendly co-parenting situation," I explained, those last words feeling funny in my mouth.

Hallie giggled. "Co-parenting is such a weird word."

"I suppose. There are married people who thought they were going to make it last forever when they had kids, and then they have nasty divorces. I can promise you this: I'm not an asshole. If we try a relationship and it doesn't work out, I'm a reasonable guy. I promise you. You can ask anybody who knows me. I'm not some jerk, and I trust that you're not either."

"You do?" She sounded doubtful.

"Yeah. I mean, hell, you're friends with your ex. That's always a good sign."

"Have you ever had a serious relationship?" she asked.

"Not since high school. I had a girlfriend then. We were 'going together,'" I said, complete with air quotes.

Hallie's lips teased with another smile. She waited for me to elaborate.

"We broke up because she moved out of town. High school is what it is. I sure thought it was going to last forever at the time, though," I offered. "Since then, I guess I just haven't settled into anything. In college, I dated here and there and had a lot of fun, but since college, I work a lot. My job doesn't lend itself to meeting someone easily. What about you?"

She shook her head quickly. "No, I also had a high school boyfriend. We both went to college in different places and grew apart. Then I had a boyfriend in college." Something dark flickered in her eyes, but it disappeared quickly. "Honestly, my friend who's having the baby with his husband, we barely dated. It's just we were close friends, so we tried to date, and it didn't work out. Probably because he's into guys, and he felt like my brother." She rolled her eyes at that.

"I'm glad it didn't ruin your friendship."

"Absolutely. He's still one of my best friends, and I'm so happy for him. I'm over my weirdness about them having a baby via a surrogate. It was just hard to learn that right around the time I was told I probably needed to get a hysterectomy." Her gaze sobered.

"That slim chance came through for you," I offered.

She nodded. "I feel lucky in a way, but it's going to throw your life into a tailspin."

"It's already happened. We're in the spin, and we'll ride it out together one way or another." She was still nestled against me, and she felt so good in my arms.

"You're a decent guy." She peered up at me, nodding firmly. "A good egg. That's what my mom would call you."

I chuckled. "Should we take a rain check for tonight?" I asked.

Her eyes held mine, and I tried to ignore the racket of my heartbeat in my chest and the need pulsing through me. I couldn't ignore how good she felt.

She took a shuddery breath, shaking her head.

"What does that mean?"

"It means I don't want to take a raincheck."

"Since we're being honest and direct, I need you to elaborate." I needed her to outline what she wanted. I didn't want to make any assumptions.

Pink crested high on her cheeks. "That night with you was amazing. It almost seems silly to try to put boundaries around it now. I mean, we've already been there and done that. You're right that there's no great time to figure this thing with us out. My gut tells me we'll be okay."

"You mean 'us'?"

"Well, I don't know if we're going to work out like as a couple, but I think we can find a way to make things work either way. If this is just some really hot chemistry we need to burn out, we might as well go ahead and take care of that, right?"

I burst out laughing, and she giggled with me. "Fair enough."

Her eyes took on a gleam, and she leaned up, tugging me down to her for another kiss. Just when I was about to lose myself in her, she broke away.

"I'm pregnant—" she began.

"I know that, Hallie."

"I know, but my body is different than it was."

Puzzled, I replied, "Uh, okay."

"My breasts are a little bigger already."

I waggled my eyebrows. "I *am* a guy."

"Oh, my god," she muttered.

Then we were kissing again, and it felt *so* fucking good. Whenever we were touching physically, Hallie shed the cloak of quiet subtlety, becoming bold and brash. Her hands mapped my chest. She slipped one under the hem of my shirt, her touch cool against my skin.

Breaking free, she murmured, "I need to see you."

Reaching behind my neck, I caught the collar of my shirt and yanked it up over my head as I leaned away. Her lips blazed a trail over my skin, and I brushed her hair back, dipping lower to nip the soft skin on the side of her neck. I loved how she shivered and arched into me with a low moan. I shifted back, lifting her away as I stood. "I need a bed. There's a bed somewhere, right?"

She giggled, turning and catching my hand in hers. She led me to her bedroom. "You don't want to make do with a couch?" she teased as she flicked the light switch and a lamp came on in the corner beside the bed.

"That one night was my best ever. After I get you out of my system, we can make do with a quickie in the living room on the couch. Right now, I want to take my time and taste every inch of you."

Her eyes went wide, and the flush on her cheeks deepened. My gaze arced around her bedroom. She had a four-poster bed with pillows piled high and a big fluffy down quilt. There was a dresser to one side and a nightstand on the other. I brought my eyes back to hers, facing her fully and cupping her cheeks as I brought my lips to hers for another lingering kiss.

I unbuttoned her blouse, letting it fall from her shoulders. My body was clamoring with need. Our clothes came off in a rush with our hands and lips mapping each other until I was down to my boxers and Hallie in a pair of blue silk panties.

We were standing at the foot of her bed, and I turned, lifting her hips onto the mattress and letting my hands rest on either side. We stared at each other. I could hear the rush of my heartbeat in my ears as everything narrowed to this moment. To nothing but us.

"What?" she whispered as I studied her.

"Just making sure you still want this."

Hallie's tongue darted out, swiping across her bottom lip. My cock, which was already swollen to the point of pain, throbbed.

"Absolutely." She closed the distance between our lips, her tongue gliding in to tease mine.

She shimmied back on the bed. I followed and shifted to her side, propping up on an elbow and glancing down. "Fuck, you're stunning, Hallie."

When my eyes made their way back to hers, she was flushed all over with her breath coming in sharp pants. I lightly cupped a breast, teasing my thumb over her swollen nipple before leaning down to suck it in. Her fingers speared my hair as she arched upward and cried out.

In all honesty, our one night before this had been so intense it was a jumble of sensations in my memory. I hadn't had time to savor her. I slid my hand over her belly, pausing to lift my head. Our eyes met, and it felt as if something shimmered in the air between us, a connection linking us. There was a baby inside her with our shared DNA. The moment was almost too intense. Her eyes broke free first, her lashes sweeping down as she took a shuddering breath.

I lost myself in her again, in need and sensation. I teased her other breast, swirling my tongue around her nipple and nipping lightly. She shivered underneath me. I cupped her mound, the silk of her panties damp against my fingers. I was impatient. As soon as I hooked my fingers to the side to find her hot, wet, and ready, I shoved her panties down. She kicked her legs, and they fell to the floor in a rumple.

Her arousal slicked my fingers, and she arched into me, her hips bucking against my touch. I shifted down, dropping kisses over her belly as she trembled. I smoothed a palm along the inside of her thigh, pressing one knee to the side. I trailed kisses along her trembling skin, and she moaned impatiently.

I dropped my mouth to the very core of her. She tasted just like I remembered, sweet and tangy with a hint of salt. With two fingers, I delved inside her, stretching her as I licked and explored every inch of her, teasing over her clit once, and then again and again and again.

I kept going until she begged, "Chase, you're teasing me," between ragged gasps.

"Sweetheart, that's the point," I said when I lifted my head.

I almost came at the sight of her. Her hair was in a tangle on the pillows. Her breasts rose and fell with every ragged breath, and her nipples were swollen and damp. She was pure woman, pure desire. We stared at each other for several beats, and again that feeling of connection shimmered. It was elemental, visceral in an elusive way. Her hips rocked again, and I dipped down, swirling my tongue around her clit and sucking on it lightly.

Her cry was a sharp, keening sound as she shuddered roughly against me. I stayed with her until the tension eased before I rose up, my eyes colliding with hers.

"I can get a condom," I said, realizing I hadn't even thought this through.

"Well, we don't need it for birth control. I can promise you I got tested for everything under the sun after my positive pregnancy test," Hallie explained. "I trust you."

"As part of our physical for work, we get

tested every year. It so happens that was a few weeks before I saw you, and I haven't been with anyone before or since."

I hadn't even let myself think about that. Not that I was all that busy sexually, but I didn't usually go for months like that. It's just I couldn't get Hallie out of my brain.

"I trust you," she whispered.

I eased my weight down over her, asking, "Is this okay?" She looked confused. "I'm not sure what's comfortable. You're pregnant," I clarified.

"It's more than okay," she said bluntly.

I held still, nudging just barely into the slick kiss of her entrance. I could feel the thud of her heartbeat against my chest, pounding in tune with mine, and then I shifted, surging into her and seating myself deeply.

My entire body strained for release, but I held tight to my control. Hallie took a breath. Letting it out, she murmured, "You feel so good."

Chapter Thirteen

HALLIE

Chase held still inside me, and I tried to breathe. The feel of him filling me was so intense I could feel myself already teetering on the edge of another climax. Pure pleasure slid through me as his dark eyes stared into mine. My heart thudded, each echoing beat feeding into the sensations coursing through me.

"Hallie," he murmured, his voice gruff and velvety.

"Chase," I returned in barely a whisper.

He dipped his head, his lips catching mine just as he drew back before filling me again. My body moved reflexively, rocking into him as he thrust into me again and again. The slick fusion of our joining was all that anchored me at this moment as I spun inside. Sensation ratcheted tighter and tighter. His angle was just so that I could feel the pressure over my clit with each surge. The pleasure felt shocking, so good I could hardly bear it. I was chasing and chasing, my release rushing at me. He shifted slightly, reaching between us, his fingers teasing over my clit. I shattered inside as I cried out, shuddering so hard my mind went blank. All I knew was he was inside me, and I was holding him fast against me.

I felt him tighten, his body bowing before he shuddered roughly, and I felt the heat of his release filling me. He shifted to the side, staying inside me as he brought me over. I fell against him. The pleasure receded slowly, like the tide rolling out on a gentle day, each wave softer and slower. My body was pinging with sensation as I tried to catch my breath.

I could hear his heart beating against my ear where my head rested on his chest. I lifted my hand, shifting to bring my palm under my chin. His gaze was bemused when his eyes opened.

"That was better than I remembered," he said. "I didn't think that was possible."

I giggled. "Me neither."

I felt the rise of his breath in his lungs. His palm shifted to slide up my spine, smoothing over my hair. I discovered I could stay there forever, relaxed and sated in Chase's arms with his dark eyes on mine.

Several moments passed before he asked, "Is this the part when I find a way to gracefully get out of bed and leave tonight?"

I didn't want him to leave. Not even a little. I shook my head and decided to be honest. "I want you to stay, but what about your dog?"

"He's with my dad. I thought that was best just in case."

"Do you do that often?"

"Only when I know I'll be gone for work. If I didn't come home tonight, I'd just tell my dad to go check on him, but I already asked."

I didn't want to admit how much I liked that. The idea he'd thought maybe he'd be staying here tonight sent a curl of warmth through me. I dipped my head, pressing a kiss at the base of his throat.

———

"Oh, my god!" I gasped as Chase filled me.

"Look at me, Hallie," he murmured.

I dragged my eyes open to find his dark gaze inches away from mine. Hot water rained down behind us as he held me in his arms. My back was pressed to the tile. We were starting our day off with shower sex.

He'd made sure we were just past the fall of water because, "Well, that messes things up," he'd teased.

He nudged deeper inside me, and I came in a shuddering rush as he followed me over the edge. None of this felt awkward with Chase. That was something I'd remembered from our first night together. Perhaps it was because I'd given myself permission to let go, to be reckless. Although the boundaries I'd placed around us that night were gone, that unspoken permission was still there.

After our shower, we got dressed. It was only after I'd been exposed and stripped bare inside and out with him that we had an actual awkward moment. It was time for him to go, and I needed to get to work for a scheduled session at my studio.

Chase stood by the door, his eyes skating over my face. "I've got the doctor's appointment in my calendar. Should I meet you there? Or should we meet here, or somewhere else, and drive over together?"

Oh, god. He was going to a doctor's appointment with me. That was how thoroughly I could forget myself with him. I'd forgotten I was pregnant. I'd forgotten we had a doctor's appointment. I hadn't *really* forgotten. Yet I'd set aside the mundane details of what it all meant. I chewed on the inside of my cheek and felt a flush rising up my neck.

He tucked his keys in his pocket and stepped in front of me, lifting a hand to palm my cheek. "What are you worrying about?" he asked.

"Now? How much time do you have?" I managed to tease lightly, relieved that he somehow sensed my anxiety and the uncertainty threatening to undo me. "Why don't you pick me up at my studio? We can meet there and ride over together."

"Sounds like a plan. Will you text me the address for your studio?"

At my nod, he leaned down. I thought he was just going to give me a quick kiss. But, oh no. Once again, he smashed my expectations to smithereens. A subtle brush of his lips over mine, a kiss at one corner of my mouth and then the other before he fit his mouth over mine in a commanding, devouring kiss. By the time he lifted his head, it was a miracle I was tingling all over and nearly a puddle at his feet.

"I'll see you then. Text me the three things."

"Huh?" My brain was mush.

"You know three favorites. We're going to know each other for a long time, Hallie. We might as well know a few more details."

My lips curled into a smile. I managed to stand there clinging to what little composure I had until the door clicked shut, and I heard his footsteps retreating across the landing and down the stairs. I leaned my back against the door, sliding my hips down to the floor, feeling as if I were melting inside and out.

"Oh, my god. Chase is dangerous," I murmured to myself as I lifted my head and thumped it against the door with a deep sigh.

Emotions twined like a vine within the intense physical sated quality I felt after last night and this morning. Chase actually seemed like a nice guy, but I didn't trust much in the world when it came to relationships.

My cell phone vibrated loudly. I stared at the coffee table before rising from the floor and crossing over to fetch my phone off it. When I lifted it and looked down, my heart seized and then lunged, casting out beats unsteadily.

I stared at the name flashing on the screen. For a moment, I was going to ignore it, but I was all about facing down the asshole on the other end of the line. Maybe it was because of what I was going through right now, but I wanted to turn the page on this chapter of my life. Sliding my thumb across the screen, I tapped to answer.

"Hello?"

"Hi, Hallie. It's Brad." As if I didn't know it was him.

"Hi, Brad." I rolled my eyes as I looked down at the screen. "What can I do for you?"

"I was wondering if we could have dinner."

I was struck speechless for a moment and simply stared at the phone. "Excuse me?" I finally said.

"Look, I understand why you might not want to, but I've actually started treatment," he explained.

"Uh, okay. What does that have to do with dinner and me?"

Brad was my only serious relationship after high school. He'd become a raging alcoholic. Now I knew, looking back, that he'd been one when I met him. I just didn't know what I was witnessing. He was one of those guys in college who partied hard, so hard that it was messy. He had a sweet side, and he came across as carefree and light when he was sober. That was the guy I'd fallen for.

Over time while we were together, it wasn't so fun anymore. I'd had a miscarriage, and that was what finally blew us apart. He thought having a baby would help him stay sober, or that was what he said when we found out I was pregnant. That was before I knew I had endometriosis, although my doctor said it was difficult to predict when it had begun.

The night I had miscarried, Brad had been out partying. I'd started bleeding and then bleeding more and more. The fact that he was calling right now nearly sent me into a panic attack. Miscarriages are awful at any time, but they're worse when you're all by yourself and scared. When I was alone and bleeding, I drove myself to the hospital, where they confirmed what was happening. An ultrasound showed the miscarriage in progress.

I'd tried in vain to call Brad, who was too drunk to answer the phone and didn't make it home for three days. That wasn't the first time that happened, but it was the last time it happened to me. We'd only spoken twice since then. Both times, he'd tried to persuade me to get back together with him. The last time had been over two years ago.

"I'm really glad you're in treatment, Brad, but I don't want to have dinner with you."

He was quiet, and I expected an argument. He surprised me when he acquiesced. "I understand. As part of my treatment, I'm trying to make amends. It's one of the twelve steps."

I bit my tongue, silently ordering myself not to be bitter. Brad used to think the twelve steps were bullshit. He'd said so many times.

"I know I used to say the twelve steps were bullshit," he said as if reading my mind. "But they're not, and they're helping me. I know I can't fix what happened, but I want you to know I'm genuinely sorry."

My heart gave an achy thump in my chest, and my throat felt thick. I blinked because I'd already cried more tears than I ever wanted over Brad. It's hard to love someone and lose them piece by piece. I'd done my own reading, and I'd even gone to Al-Anon. I knew the man I'd loved wasn't the man who fell further down the slope of alcohol. All the parts I hated were the addiction, but it didn't change that he was still responsible for his own actions.

"I appreciate that, Brad," I finally said when I could get a breath in.

"I'm not going to try to persuade you to get back together with me," he added. "I should have been there for you when you had the miscarriage. I'm so sorry you lost our baby alone. I'm trying to forgive myself, but that's the heaviest weight."

I was pretty sure he meant it, but it hurt to hear. I steeled myself and took a quiet breath, keeping my tears in check. "Thank you."

"Still no dinner?"

Of course, he had to push a little. "No, I appreciate the phone call. I appreciate the apology. I think you need to figure this out on your own. I can't be there for you for this. I can tell you that I care about you, and I always will. You can know that I am cheering you on in the background."

I swallowed, and it hurt. Even though I told myself I'd already said goodbye to Brad, letting go of Brad when he wasn't drunk or hungover and in denial about his issues was different. There was a finality to it that hadn't existed before.

"Thank you, Hallie. Thanks for even answering the phone," he said somberly.

"Of course. If I see you, I'll always be glad to see you. Stay in that program and don't start another relationship just to escape."

His chuckle was dry. "You know me well, Hallie."

"I know I do. You can do this. I believe you can."

"I've been sober for eight months now."

I almost dropped the phone. "Wow," I finally said. "I'm impressed. You should be proud of yourself."

"I am. It's not easy, but I'm trying."

"You take care, Brad."

"You too, Hallie. If you ever need me, just call."

"Thank you." I managed to keep my voice level even though I knew I'd never call him.

When I hung up the phone, I started crying. It felt like a dam had suddenly broken open in my chest. I cried and cried in a way I hadn't cried since the first few months after the miscarriage, which had been years ago at this point. At first, I'd been numb, just trying to put one foot in front of the other and get through each day. I'd managed only the required tasks—breathing, brushing my teeth, taking showers, getting dressed, working, pasting on a polite smile at gallery showings and jobs for photo shoots. Those actions had been the scaffolding that had held me up when everything felt like it was falling apart inside. The simple act of living was a Hail

Mary pass of hope when emotionally it hurt to be alive. Maybe after six months or so, the veil of numbness started to lift, and I'd cried a lot at night when I was alone.

I'd been angry, furious, and grieving. Right around then, they discovered my first ovarian cyst and then the next and the first surgery and so on and so forth. Brad calling tonight brought it all rushing back.

I cried to the point I was hiccupping. My phone rang again.

Chapter Fourteen

HALLIE

I sighed, swiping the heels of my palms across my cheeks before glancing down at the screen. My brother's name flashed.

I tapped the screen to answer. "Hey, Darren," I said, hoping my tears weren't obvious in my voice.

"Hey, are you crying?" he asked immediately.

I rolled my eyes, grateful he couldn't see me. "No," I lied. "I just came in. It's windy out."

"Ah," he replied. "Risa said you wanted to talk to me."

I silently groaned. I'd asked Risa to let Darren know I wanted to chat. I was grateful she'd given him the pregnancy news to give him time to adjust. I hadn't asked her to keep the news to herself because I doubted Risa could keep a secret like that from my brother.

"Yeah," I said, thinking it was just going to be that kind of day. "Well, like Risa told you, I'm pregnant."

The line went so quiet, I prompted, "Darren, are you there?"

"Yeah, I'm here," he said, his tone sharp. "Risa told me. Is this good news or bad news?"

"It's good news."

"Congratulations then," he said.

I could practically picture my brother's face. He wouldn't know how to reply. He did know about my reproductive issues, so to speak. Risa had come to stay with me after my miscarriage, and they both knew about my surgeries.

"I'll just give you all the details," I forged ahead. "No, I haven't been in a serious relationship. This is completely unexpected. We used condoms. The father is stepping up. He wants to be involved, and I'm having the baby."

Darren fell silent again. I thought he was probably clenching his teeth because I knew my brother well. He liked when things stayed neat and tidy in life. I was not neat and tidy, or rather, this situation wasn't. While he appreciated my photography, he didn't appreciate me working as a freelancer. He worried about my benefits, my stability, my income, and so on.

"You'll be glad to learn the father is a firefighter. He's a hotshot out of Willow Brook."

"Okay?"

"Sheesh, I thought you'd be glad to hear that. Doesn't that mean he's stable?"

"Well, no, not necessarily," Darren countered.

"Why not? He's got a full-time job and I'm sure he has good benefits."

"Probably. But hotshot firefighting isn't the most stable career. It's pretty risky."

"You do it," I retorted.

While my brother was a police chief, he was also trained as a firefighter and helped out in a pinch with the crews down in Diamond Creek on occasion.

"Fair enough. I'm sorry if that came out a little judgmental."

"Just a little," I replied, my tone dry. I loved my brother, but he could play the stereotype like nobody else when it came to being a little overprotective.

"You have to admit this is a lot of news for me to absorb."

"I will definitely agree with that."

Darren chuckled, and I could hear Risa's voice in the background. "What did Risa say? Did she tell you to be nice?" I teased.

"Yes," he muttered, sounding chastised. "I thought you were about to schedule surgery."

"Yeah, I was, and that's something to consider later. Right now, I'm pregnant, and the baby is healthy. Everything's going very well. I really want this to be okay, Darren." Tears were salty in my throat.

"I know, and I know you're worried," he said, his tone softening.

"My doctor is great, and I'm just going to hope it will be okay because that's all I can do."

"I hope so too. Do you mind giving me this guy's name?"

"Oh, my god, Darren. You can't look him up," I ordered even though I'd been planning to ask my brother to look him up if I hadn't been able to track him down myself. "Come on, you know they did a background check on him. He's a hotshot firefighter."

"How did you meet this guy, Hallie?"

There was *no* way in hell I was about to

fess up to those details with my older brother.

"Look, I met him when I was out one night. One of his friends vouched for him," I explained.

"And you know his friend well?" my suspicious brother pressed.

Okay, so I'd only met Delilah twice. Maybe I'd been in her presence for a half an hour, tops. I wasn't going to go into that with my brother. It made me feel small, ridiculous, and foolish. I didn't need to tumble into a vortex of negative feelings. I was having this baby and hoped and prayed the universe had slipped me a good card after a few shitty ones in the deck of life.

I heard Darren take a deep breath and realized I hadn't responded yet. "Darren, calm down. I'm not dating an alcoholic anymore," I said flatly, well aware of how he'd felt about Brad and that disaster of a relationship.

"I guess that's a good point. But do you know this guy's not an alcoholic?"

I didn't, but I was pretty sure he wasn't. I was hyperaware of the signs of someone who drank too much. Chase hadn't even missed a beat at his choice to abstain from alcohol while I did during my pregnancy. "I don't think so," was all I could muster.

"What's his name?"

I bit back a sigh. It wasn't like I could hide this information from Darren. "Chase Mills. He's from Willow Brook, Alaska. He grew up there. He has one sister, his mother passed away, and his father still lives in Willow Brook. As I said, he's a hotshot firefighter on one of the crews there."

"That's enough information. I'll see what I can find out," my brother replied.

"Don't do anything weird, Darren," I ordered through gritted teeth.

"I'm not going to do anything weird. Just because he has a respectable job doesn't mean he's a respectable guy. Hell, I know plenty of cops who have their own records. Just let me check on him. You're having a baby with this guy."

"I am." I wanted to feel confident and positive about this. I wanted to will this pregnancy to go well.

"I know Rex Masters up there. He's the police chief in Willow Brook. I'm going to give him a call. He'll give me the off-the-record scoop."

"Fine," I muttered, knowing I couldn't stop my brother.

"When did you tell Risa?"

"Oh, my god! She told you, so why does it

matter? I didn't ask her to keep it a secret, so I'm guessing she told you right off."

Darren's chuckle was warm. "She wants to talk to you, so I'll hand the phone over. I love you."

"I love you too."

"If I find out anything—"

I cut him off. "You'll tell me. Thanks for doing something I didn't even ask."

He was grumbling as he passed the phone to Risa.

"Hey, girl," she said as soon as she got on the line.

"Hey. How's he looking? Tense and worried?"

She laughed. "He'll be fine. He's still adjusting to the news. How's it going with Chase?"

"Well, we had dinner."

"How did that go?"

"He stayed the night."

"Oh, so it went well then?"

"That's one way of putting it," I replied, my cheeks burning up.

Her sly laughter filtered through the line. "Let me know how your doctor's appointment goes. If you need anything—"

"I know. You'll be there."

"Of course, I will. We're family. Cell phone fist bump."

I laughed, lifting my fist in the air and tapping it at an imaginary fist. "Talk soon, all right?"

I set my phone down and leaned back, sliding my hand over my belly. I kept waiting to feel movement. On occasion, I did, but it was subtle. My doctor kept telling me not to worry too much.

But still, I worried.

Chapter Fifteen

CHASE

"What do you think?" Rhys Cannon asked.

I leaned back, adjusting my earbuds and drumming my fingertips on the kitchen table. I was having my second conversation with my half brother.

"I'd love to come down there," I finally said.

I wasn't sure "love" was the accurate word, but I was willing to try to build this bridge to my half siblings. It was probably the only way I could somehow get to know the father who had passed away before I even knew he was my father.

"It's an open invitation. Our family owns plenty of properties down here. You can have one of the guesthouses all to yourself. That way, we won't crowd you," Rhys explained. "I have to admit, there are a lot of us."

"No shit," I said with a dry chuckle.

I had seven—seven!—half siblings. It was enough to wrap my brain around that, but even more complicated, my biological father's family was wealthy. Seriously wealthy. I thought about my friend Archer, who'd turned out to be my cousin, and how he'd assured me my newly discovered family was a good bunch.

"I swear we're not awful," Rhys continued. "We might be a little annoying. You can ask Archer. You guys grew up together, right?"

"We went to elementary school together before his family moved. It's good to have him back in town."

"Archer's a good guy," Rhys commented.

"He is," I agreed.

I sensed Rhys wanted this to work out. But we didn't know each other.

"Well, you know where to reach me. I've texted you everybody's phone number. You can call any of us at any time. If it'd be more comfortable for one of us to come there and meet on your turf, I'm happy to do it."

"I know. I just need to figure out the timing."

"All right. Talk soon."

"You got it."

We ended the call, and I took a deep breath. Fuck. This was weird. My relationship with my mother was complicated even after her death. She had been this bright force. I'd desperately wanted to please her when I was little, but there was no pleasing her. She was flighty with a hard edge and a wildness to her. As an adult, I could see how my father fell for her and probably how my biological father fell for her. She could be charming beyond belief.

Yet whenever I thought of her, there was a sense of emptiness, of always reaching for something that was never there. After she'd passed away, I tried to accept that the love I'd always chased after from her was never going to be caught. Then come to find out she'd lied to me, my father, and my sister for my entire life. Because of that lie, I lost the chance to even know my biological father. I felt conflicted that I even wanted to know who I was because I genuinely loved my dad. He was the father of my heart and my soul.

My eyes lifted to the clock mounted above the kitchen doorway. I was about to be late for dinner with my dad.

———

"So what'll it be?" the server asked, her eyes flicking back and forth between my dad and me.

"Gracie, I think I'll take that salmon burger. You promise it's good?" my dad asked.

Gracie clucked as she nodded. "Of course, it's good."

"All right, I'll go with that."

"I'll take the same," I added. "I'd also like those sweet potato fries, the spicy ones."

"Oh, good lord, don't give me those. I want the plain fries," my dad chimed in.

Gracie cast him a smile. "I know you don't like spicy. I'm amazed you'll even try a salmon burger."

"Of course, I'll try salmon. I'm Alaskan born and bred."

She chuckled. "Anything to drink, guys?"

"I'll take a pint of the house draft," I replied.

"Same." My dad nodded.

Gracie smiled between us. "Like father, like son."

My dad winked at her as she hurried away.

"You just can't not flirt," I commented dryly.

He winked at me. "I've known Gracie since she was in diapers. That wasn't flirting."

Just then, Rex Masters paused by the table with his wife, Georgia.

"Hey, Rex," my dad said.

I smiled up at him. "Good to see you, Rex. How's it going, Georgia?"

Her eyes twinkled with her smile. "Pretty good."

"Having a father-son dinner?" Rex asked.

I felt a little twist in my heart. Ever since I'd learned the truth about my family, it felt as if someone had shafted a thin knife in my heart. Not deep enough to kill me, just deep enough to hurt like hell.

My dad and I usually had dinner every other week or so. It wasn't a hard and fast schedule. We'd always had a tight relationship. My father hadn't even known the truth either, and it didn't bother him. He didn't even give a damn. He'd asked more than once, "Why does it change anything? I'm your father in every way that matters."

It explained a lot about my mom. But then again, maybe not really. It wasn't as if her lying was a shock. She went through most of her life lying and charming.

"Yep," my dad was saying. "Just like you and Cade."

Cade and I had grown up together. With his father the police chief in Willow Brook and Cade one of the superintendents on one of the hotshot crews at Willow Brook Fire & Rescue, I saw them both almost daily.

"How's your grandbaby?" my dad asked.

A wide smile cracked across Rex's face. "Right as rain."

"Being a grandpa suits him," Georgia said.

"Well, doesn't being a grandma suit you?" my dad teased.

She smiled warmly. "Sure does. It's the best of both worlds. We get to fuss over them, love them, and spoil them, but we also get to sleep through the night."

My dad chuckled, and I thought about the fact that he was going to love being a granddad.

"Well, we're heading home," Rex commented. "Just stopped to say hi. Good to see you two."

"Same. You coming to cards this week?" my dad asked.

Rex nodded. "You bet."

An older group of men in town had been playing cards together for decades. They alternated locations and kept the betting pool low. "Next Wednesday, right?" Rex prompted.

"You got it. My place," my dad replied.

At that, Rex and Georgia waved and started walking, pausing again to greet somebody at another table. A few minutes later, after our beers had been served, I took a breath, deciding to just dive right in.

"Well, Dad, on the topic of being a grandparent," I began.

My dad's brows hitched up. "Yeah?"

"I'm about to be a father."

"Come again?" my dad countered with a big smile. "I didn't even know you had a girlfriend."

"Well, uh, I didn't. There's no easy way to put this, but I met a woman four months ago. She's pregnant."

My dad chuckled, the sound low and raspy. "Well, well. It sounds like that was a good night."

"Seriously, Dad?" I countered with a groan.

He rolled his eyes. "Do you know her well?"

"No, not really," I said honestly. "But she found me when she realized she was pregnant."

"I take it she's planning on keeping the baby."

"Yep. That's why she came to find me."

"Congratulations. How do you feel about it?"

I took a swallow of beer, conducting a mental scan of my body, heart, and soul. "Well, I think I'm all right. I'm still dealing with the shock of it, but I'm ready."

"Do you like her?"

"I do. Her brother is the police chief in Diamond Creek."

"Ah. Well, you might as well get the scoop on him from Rex," my dad said matter-of-factly.

I shook my head slowly as I laughed. "Figured you'd say that."

"Nothing wrong with doing a little reconnaissance. She's about to be the mother of your son."

"I know, but I trust her, Dad. My gut has a good feeling," I insisted.

"You know, son, gut feelings aren't always right."

Given the news bomb my family had absorbed recently, that was a practical point.

"Tell me seriously, Dad. You have always been very circumspect about Mom, and I respect that you never wanted to bash her even though we didn't have a good relationship. Tell me the truth. We obviously all know now that she was pregnant with Jacob Cannon's baby when you married her."

My dad took a deep breath. "Son, it doesn't matter all that much."

"It does to me," I pressed, my voice low. I just want to understand why you married her."

"Because I wanted to be your father. My gut feeling wasn't wrong about your mom. She was like a flame that burned fast. She was impossible to look away from."

"I know."

"And when she came to me and told me she was pregnant, the timeline was vague. There was a seed of doubt in the corner of my mind that maybe I wasn't the only guy she'd been with. But I was stable. I'm kind of a boring guy."

"Dad, you're not boring," I insisted.

"You know what I mean. I don't party. My adrenaline comes from being outdoors, but that's about it. I was born and raised here. I was financially stable, and I already owned my own home. I knew I could be a good father, and I wanted children, so I chose to believe her. Then we had your sister. I had a family, and I loved you both so much. In a way, I loved your mother. She was not a perfect person, but none of us are."

"Dad, Mom was something different than not perfect. She was toxic."

My father took a deep breath, letting it out before taking a swallow from his beer. "I recognize that's how you feel, and I wish things had been different. She was a wounded person, and she hurt other people as she went through life, including you and your sister."

My throat ached. That splinter lodged in my heart stung.

"Life is never easy. That's one thing I know. Maybe it was a mistake to make the call I did, but you were coming along no matter what. She was also your mother, and that wasn't going to change. I love you *as* my son, not like a son. You *are* my son."

My father thumped his fist against his chest, his eyes glistening as he held my gaze. He leaned across the table, uncurling his palm and clasping my shoulder. He squeezed firmly, his touch steadying me inside. "It's gonna be okay. I am sorry that she lied, and I'm sorry that it hurt you. I wish I'd known sooner. Your bio dad sounds like a good man. We would have been friends."

I took a shaky breath and nodded.

"I've held back out of respect for you, but don't turn away your family. Family is what you make it. I know that for a fact, whether it's blood or something else, the ties that bind are the ties that bind. The ties that we strengthen become stronger. They want to know you, so give them that chance."

"Fuck, Dad. You're gonna make me cry in a fucking restaurant," I muttered hoarsely.

He chuckled. "All right. Enough of the deep talk. Think about it, though. Your sister wants to be that bridge. You know her. She loves building bridges."

"I know she does."

"We can't change what happened, but you can change how you deal with it," he said firmly.

I took another shaky breath. "I love you, Dad."

"And I love you, son."

I took a swallow of beer and gulped in air. I let it out slowly, and the tightness in my throat started to ease. I blinked back the tears just before Gracie arrived with our salmon burgers.

"Okay, guys, anything else?" she asked with a smile.

"Nope. We're all set."

My dad was true to his word because he was that kind of man. We moved on from the deep talk and chatted about his guiding schedule for the summer.

When I got home that night, I pulled out my phone and tapped out a text to Hallie.

Me: *Told my dad. He's really excited.*

Hallie: *Great! We haven't done our three things today. What are your three favorite fishing spots in Alaska?*

Me: *Is this a trick question?*

Locals in Alaska could be *seriously* opinionated about fishing spots.

Hallie: *No! I figure you're informed because your dad's a guide.*

I grinned as I replied.

Me: *Well, are we talking salmon or halibut? If salmon, are we talking rod fishing or dipnetting? The details matter, you know.*

HALLIE

I was beyond nervous. My stomach felt like it was flipping in my belly, and I honestly couldn't tell if I was actually feeling my baby move or if I was just *that* nervous about Chase arriving to meet me for my doctor's appointment.

The other night with him had been good. Almost too good. I'd been dreaming of him and dreaming of our baby and starting to get hopes that were crazy. Super domestic. Visions of me cooking dinner, us having a big house and a whole passel of kids, a dog, and maybe a cat, or a bearded dragon. All these wildly overblown thoughts all because Chase said he wanted to see how things go with us.

That didn't mean we were going to fall in love. That was the problem.

I was really, *really* falling for him.

But you've only had two nights with him. It's just the sex. You can't even think straight.

I couldn't ruminate or obsess any further. In all honesty, I'd obsessed for hours upon hours upon hours. There was a knock on my door, and I stared at it from where I sat on the couch. I'd texted him to pick me up here instead of at my studio because my schedule had changed.

I stood, smoothing my hands over my belly where the curve was starting to show more by the day. I crossed the room, stopping by the door. I took a deep breath and let it out slowly, willing my pulse to slow the hell down.

He knocked again, and I laughed to myself. I swung the door open quickly. "Hey!" I practically yelped.

His eyes widened slightly. "Hey, Hallie." His gaze skated over my face, dipping down to my belly and then back up. I felt my cheeks heating. "How are you?"

"Uh, just nervous actually," I blurted out, not intending to be that blunt.

His eyes warmed. "Well, that makes two of us then."

"Oh, you're nervous too?"

"Yeah. I've never been to a doctor's appointment with a woman. I have no idea what to expect. And obviously, I've never been a father. So this is all new for me."

We laughed together. He stepped closer, lifting a hand and brushing some loose locks of hair off my cheek as he bent low to brush a kiss over my lips. "Good to see you," he murmured.

It literally felt as if hot cinders fell through me. My whole body felt tingly with sparks of heat.

"Should we go?" he asked.

I nodded quickly.

"Should we drive?"

I shook my head. "No, let's walk. It's just a few blocks away."

The next thing I knew, we were walking down the sidewalk, and Chase was holding my hand. His grip was firm and warm, his palm dry.

"How was your drive?" I heard myself asking politely.

"Good. I always like the drive to Anchorage."

"Really?"

"Yeah, it's a pretty drive. Anchorage is a

city, but it's a stunning view all the way here from Willow Brook."

I smiled up at him. "True." I looked ahead again. "Here we are." I stopped in front of the sign at my doctor's office. I hadn't even been thinking about it, but I suddenly realized I needed to tell him about my miscarriage. It wasn't as if I'd been hiding it, it's just it was a sad, painful time in my life. I cleared my throat, peering up at him. "I need to tell you something."

His brows hitched up as he nodded. I gulped in a quick breath of air, trying to ignore the tightness in my chest. "I had a miscarriage a few years ago."

He was dead silent for long enough I started to worry. Until his eyes skated over my face, concern held there. "Okay. I'm sorry."

I blinked away the tears stinging my eyes. "Thank you. I, uh... Well, you already know I have endometriosis, and they don't know if that affected my pregnancy then. Anyway, it was with an ex who turned out to be an alcoholic. We broke up, and that's long over, but I guess I thought you should know." I gestured toward the entrance to the doctor's office. "I don't know why I'm telling you now. It just felt like I should."

He studied me for another moment. The feel of his thumb brushing in a gentle path over the inside of my wrist was comforting. "Okay. You didn't have to tell me."

The tightness is my chest was easing, and I took a full breath. "I know, but I wanted to. I promise I'm not all hung up on it."

He nodded again, and I just felt—okay. That was all I needed.

A moment later, we were walking in, and the receptionist smiled at me, her eyes bouncing curiously to Chase.

"I'm here for my appointment. Hallie Thomas."

"Yep. Just a sec. Let me check you in." She typed on her keyboard. "Any updates for insurance?"

"No changes."

"Okay, have a seat. Dr. Williams will be with you shortly."

We sat down, and I looked around. At the moment, no one else was waiting. Chase glanced over at the magazine rack and then back at me. "Wow."

"Wow, what?"

"It's all parenting or health magazines. These aren't the kind of magazines I see in my doctor's office."

I burst out laughing. "It's usually women here unless they're bringing a guy with them."

Just then, the door to the back hallway where all the offices were opened, and my doctor peered out. "Hey, Hallie. Come on back." She waved us toward her.

We stood together. I didn't know what to think about the fact that I reached for Chase's hand, relieved to discover he was reaching for me at the same time. My doctor's eyes dipped down to our clasped hands when we approached her.

"This is Chase," I said.

She held a computer tablet in her hands and dipped her chin in a nod. "Nice to meet you, Chase. I'm Dr. Williams."

Chase smiled. "Nice to meet you too."

"Come on back," she added as she turned to lead us down the hallway.

My heart was thumping hard in my chest. It was weird to have a baby inside me. For my entire life, I was accustomed to feeling my own body have reactions. Now, whenever something happened, I felt like I could also feel my baby's response. The rush of blood felt different through my system. We walked down the hallway, which had cream-colored walls and soothing watercolor paintings. Our footfalls were muted on the thin carpeting.

Dr. Williams turned into a doorway, and we walked into the exam room. "Here we go. So let's have a seat first."

Chase and I sat together on the only two chairs against the wall, and she sat on a low stool that had an attached desk with a computer screen mounted on it. She set her tablet down and shifted the computer screen to look at it before smiling.

"Chase is the father," I said quickly.

"Okay. I'm glad you're here. How do you two want to handle this appointment? I need to do an exam. Do you want him in here for that? He can be here for the whole thing if you'd like."

"That's fine," I said quickly. I'd already thought this part through. We'd had sex. This was no big deal.

Dr. Williams nodded. "We're going to do the ultrasound so you can find out the baby's gender."

"Today?" I squeaked. "We thought there would be an official appointment for that."

She smiled. "I mentioned it, but it's possible you have a lot on your mind and it didn't sink in," she explained with a warm smile before adding, "You're eighteen weeks along now. The big question is do you two want to know your baby's gender? Have you had this conversation?"

"Yes. We decided we want to know," I said. We'd had that convo via text with a phone follow-up, and I was grateful we'd thought ahead.

She smiled. "Okay. That's a relief. I don't mind keeping the secret, but it's nice when I don't have to worry about it. Every so often, I've slipped up by accident." Chase grinned. "It's not like I announce it. I have to be careful to call the baby, the baby all the time. This makes it easier. All right, well, let me go over what we do at these upcoming appointments. As long as Hallie wants you here, you are welcome at any of the appointments, but I'll always defer to her."

"Completely understood," Chase said with a nod.

"They're kind of boring. This is the most exciting one," she offered.

"Any appointment Hallie invites me to, I'll be here," Chase said firmly. "I respect that it's her call."

"Good. We're all on the same page." She quickly summarized the basics of the appointments and the schedule before finishing with, "Now, I'm going to step out. Hallie, you can change into a gown and get comfortable on the table. The ultrasound machine is right in here. We'll do the whole thing together."

After she left, Chase asked, "Are you sure you want me to stay?"

"Definitely. You've seen me naked," I teased.

"Uh, I think this is different. It doesn't feel very sexy," he said as he looked around the room.

I burst out laughing as I stood. I quickly stripped down and pulled on the gown keeping on my socks because the room was chilly.

"Nice socks," he said with a grin.

I looked down at my feet. I was wearing a pair of alternating striped pink and purple socks. "Thank you. I like to keep my socks fun. Might as well." I sat on the table, swinging my legs.

"Do we do anything?" he asked.

"No, she'll knock in a second."

As if on cue, a light knock sounded on the door. "Ready?" she called, her voice muffled through the door.

"Yeah, come on in."

She came in and did the exam. When she smeared the ultrasound jelly on my belly, I commented, "Ooh, that's warm."

"I know. I love it. It's made a big difference for patients."

"What's that?" Chase asked when she whipped out the wand.

She grinned. "It's a wand with a camera on it. "It helps me see."

"You don't do this on her belly?" he asked, his eyes widening.

"We actually do both. There's a camera on this and on that," she explained, gesturing to the wand and then the smaller handheld tool.

"Holy shit," he said. "That's kind of weird and invasive."

Dr. Williams burst out laughing. "I appreciate your bluntness, and I agree. At the moment, it's the only way to do it, so here we go. Your job is to look at the screen."

Chase was completely fascinated by the process. I liked how interested he was. She explained everything thoroughly. "You two ready for the big reveal?"

"Sure," I replied just as Chase said, "For sure."

"Is it 100 percent?" he asked.

"It's 99 percent accurate at this stage in the pregnancy."

A moment later, she said, "Looks like you have a baby boy on the way."

"Oh, my god," I breathed.

Tears rolled down my cheeks, and Chase was hugging me. It was all a little overwhelming. Dr. Williams shifted back to business pretty quickly, interjecting, "You two can stay in here for a bit, but I have another appointment. Everything looks great, and your baby boy is on schedule so far."

She removed the wand from inside me, wiped the jelly off my belly, and I sat up on the table. "You are totally on track. Next up is the testing. That can be stressful, so I just want to prepare you. Some people choose not to do it."

"We're doing it. We've already had the conversation," I announced.

That was one of the weirdest things about this with Chase. Even though we were fresh and this was crazy, I had felt the need to be transparent about everything. We weren't skipping any of the hard conversations.

She nodded. "Okay, then."

"You'll see us both," I said firmly.

She smiled. "Schedule your next appointment on the way out and see you soon. Very nice to meet you," she said to Chase just before she hurried away.

I got dressed quickly. Chase looked over at me. "What do we do now?" he asked.

"We go out, and I schedule my next appointment. You might as well pull up your work schedule, so we can figure out what works for you."

"Damn, this is weird," Chase said as we walked down the hallway a minute later. "How do you feel?"

My heart was pounding in this crazy, joyous beat, and I was almost overwhelmed with emotion. "I feel *a lot*," I said honestly.

He chuckled. "That makes two of us."

Chapter Seventeen

CHASE

I hadn't planned on spending the night with Hallie, but I did. It seemed nothing that happened with her was planned. While nothing was planned, everything felt imbued with meaning and emotion that was startling in its intensity.

We went to lunch after her appointment. No big deal, except I couldn't keep my eyes off her mouth and couldn't stop thinking about kissing her and wanting the feel of her skin against mine. She asked what I was doing for the rest of the day.

That evening as we were about to leave for dinner with her parents, her lashes swept down as a flush bloomed across her cheeks. "Chase," she whispered. When her eyes opened again, her gaze locked onto mine with such force, I couldn't look away even if I tried. "Why? Why do I feel like this with you?"

My heart thumped in recognition of her question. My heart was asking the same thing. All I wanted to do was keep her close.

"I don't know," I murmured, lightly dragging my knuckles across her collarbone. Her skin was warm, and I watched as the flush deepened on her cheeks. "I'd ask the same of you. Do you know the answer?"

She shook her head, her hair shifting with the motion. I slid my hand through those silky locks and dipped my head to fit my mouth over hers. She breathed in sharply, the sound of the hitch in her throat sizzling through my system.

We were by her door, and she spun me, boldly pushing me back until my shoulders bumped into the wall. Her naughty, deft fingers flicked the buttons of my fly. She broke free of our kiss, shimmying down. Her palm stroked boldly over the hard and swollen ridge of my arousal.

"Don't we have to go?" I asked between gritted teeth.

That glint in her eyes was sly and naughty,

and my balls tightened, my release already threatening.

"We have a few minutes," she teased.

My cock sprang free when she shoved my boxers down. Her tongue dragged in a slow tease along the underside of my cock before she swiped up the bead of precum rolling out the tip.

With my jaw clenching as I scrambled for restraint, my hands slapped against the wall. I tried to protest, but I couldn't even muster a word. I felt the warm, slick kiss of her mouth closing around me when she sucked me inside. My head thumped against the wall as I clung to my control.

She sucked me in deeply and rocked back on her heels when she drew away. Her lashes lifted as she stared up at me for a moment. Her lips were kiss bitten, her eyes dark with passion. I almost came right then. She smiled as she leaned forward again, drawing me in as her palm curled around my length. Another moment later, my release was spurting into her mouth, whipping through me with such force that I was grateful for the wall behind me.

Hallie shifted back, slowly releasing me. I dragged my eyes open when I felt her tugging my boxers back into place and buttoning my jeans.

"Fuck, Hallie." My voice came out in a ragged gasp.

"Later," she teased.

I gave my head a shake, resting against the wall for another few moments to catch my breath as pleasure echoed in electric swirls through my body. A few minutes later, we were in my truck, and I glanced over.

"I don't feel right about that," I said.

"What do you mean? I'm pregnant with your baby. By the way, it's not like we haven't done that before," she pointed out, her tone dry.

"I know, but you're taking me to meet your parents," I protested.

She shrugged. "They know I'm pregnant."

"Did they know you were planning to invite me over tonight?"

"I hadn't really thought ahead. They're pretty easygoing. It'll be fine. I texted and told them you were in town."

I paused before turning out of the parking area behind her building onto the street. "I hope so. I haven't met anyone's parents since my high school girlfriend."

The look in her eyes was reassuring when I slid my gaze sideways. "Don't look so stressed out. We're having a baby together. No matter what, you're going to see them."

I took a breath, trying to ignore the nervousness tightening in my chest. "I know. My dad would like to meet you, and so would my sister."

"Oh, wow. Now I understand why you're nervous," she said.

I burst out laughing.

———

"Nice to meet you," Hallie's father said, his handshake firm. Anthony dipped his head with a quick smile.

"Nice to meet you as well," I returned as he released my hand.

"This is my mom, Pam," Hallie offered.

Pam smiled at me, her eyes warm. Her hair was the same shade of soft brown as Hallie's and streaked with silver. Her father's hair was all white, but she had his eyes, although hers had more green in the hazel swirl.

"It's so nice to meet you," her mother added.

This was awkward. I was the father to be, and I'd never even met her parents before. As the evening passed, I discovered Hallie was right. They were pretty easygoing. I could tell her father was sizing me up, but he wasn't an asshole about it. Apparently, he knew my dad.

"He took me out on a hunt," Anthony said.

"Ah, I hope it was a good one," I replied.

"Of course, it was. I was bringing a friend from out of state, so I preferred to have a professional guide. I like your dad because he's not too tough guy about it."

I chuckled. "I know what you mean."

Backcountry guides tended to slot into two categories—either the highly skilled and practical ones like my father, or the potentially highly skilled, or maybe not, but arrogant ones. It was hit or miss.

"You enjoy firefighting?" he asked.

"I do. I like being out in the wilderness. It's not something I can do forever, but I plan to do it as long as I can." As soon as I spoke, I silently cursed.

Her father probably wondered about me actually providing for Hallie and our baby.

"What do you plan to do after that?" he asked.

"I could do guiding like my father, but by the time I'm ready to take a break from firefighting, I'm not sure I'll want to travel that much. I got a degree in business when I went to college."

"Practical choice and gives you options," he returned.

"I am a planner," I said with a wry smile.

It was only after Hallie went with her mother to look at something in the garage that her father studied me carefully. I braced myself.

"Hallie tells me you're stepping up to the plate."

"Yes, sir," I said. "I take my responsibilities seriously. When Hallie told me she was pregnant, I told her I'd support whatever she wanted to do, and I will. It's important to me to be involved, and I care about Hallie."

Her father nodded slowly. "Okay then. Doesn't seem like you two have been involved for very long."

I shook my head. "We haven't." I wasn't going to lie, even if a tiny part of me thought that might make this easier.

"She really wants children," he said.

"I understand. I do too. Maybe this didn't happen in a planned way, but I don't think that changes the outcome."

Her father eyed me, pressing his tongue in his cheek before adding, "She's always traveled a lot. It'll be good for her to be in one place."

"Okay," I replied, not sure what else to say.

His eyes held mine, and I felt as if he were peeling back the layers of my brain. "I'm glad you're going to be there for her. Please let us know if you need anything."

I breathed a silent sigh of relief when Hallie and her mother reappeared.

Later when we were back at Hallie's place and she was curled up against my side with her fingertip tracing slow circles on my chest, she asked, "Was it so bad?" Her voice was a low rasp in the darkness.

"No, your parents are really nice. They seem easygoing like you said."

I thought about what I told her father and the bulwark of baggage behind what it meant for me to be part of my child's life. It was the right thing to do, to be there as a father for any child of mine. But for me, there was so much more to it than that.

"How about you come to Willow Brook next weekend? We can have dinner with my father, and hopefully, my sister can make it to town for the weekend."

"Okay," Hallie whispered.

She dusted a kiss on my shoulder, shifting

slightly against me. Only seconds later, her breath evened out.

In my heart, I knew I was falling for Hallie, and I didn't know what to do about it. Even though I was the one who had said we might as well see where this takes us, I hadn't thought it through. I'd been acting on this hazy concept of trusting the chemistry.

I couldn't help but wonder what her father had meant about her traveling. I didn't have a problem with that. I traveled plenty, but I was trying to read between the lines of her father's comment and worried maybe Hallie didn't want to settle down. I'd always told myself I would know if I met someone who shared any qualities with my mother. My mother had taken flighty to extremes, and she'd traveled frequently. She was flighty about what she wore. In a single hour before she went somewhere, she was constantly changing, and her moods shifted quicker than the wind during a storm.

I told myself I was creating things to worry about. I smoothed my hand through Hallie's hair and told my doubts to shut the hell up.

Chapter Eighteen

CHASE

"You got that?" Graham called.

I glanced over, lifting up the hook he'd just tossed to me. "Got it."

We kept walking, the frosty ground crunching under our boots. It was spring in Alaska but still thawing in the northern parts of the state. We were returning from a training exercise, which also served to put out a fire. This had been a small one set by the landowner. They'd been burning brush in a burn barrel and left it unattended for too long. The wind tossed some sparks into a dry area, and poof, we had a fire. These were the easy days—fly in, put out a fire, and fly out.

"How's it going?" Rowan asked when I

stopped by where some of our crew was seated on fallen logs.

We were waiting for the helicopter that was on its way to pick us up. "Good, easy day. I like a challenge too, but I don't mind this."

"These are what I call hero days," Graham commented as he stopped beside me.

"Hero days?" Rowan prompted.

"Yeah, we fly in and put the fire out inside of a few hours." He lifted an arm, flexing his muscles.

"Makes sense," I replied with a chuckle.

Rowan handed me a bottle of water, and I took a few swallows before sitting down beside him on the log. He finished a bite of a granola bar before asking, "So are the rumors true?"

"What rumors?"

"That you're going to be a father."

I almost choked on the sip of water I'd just taken. After sputtering and taking a breath, I caught his eyes and nodded. "Yes, but how the hell did you know?"

"Well, you told your father who told Mae's father. Of course, he told Mae's mother who told Mae, and then she told me," Rowan offered dryly. "It's a small town. I'm sure your father told somebody else."

"Dude, everybody knows," Graham chimed in. "Can't keep a secret around here."

I groaned, propping my elbows on my knees and glancing amongst my crew members and friends.

"How do you feel?" Graham prompted.

"Still getting used to the idea, but pretty good. I think," I said slowly.

"Having a baby is no joke," Graham offered. "And on the unplanned pregnancy front, at least you're older than I was."

I burst out laughing. "Dude, you got a girl pregnant when we were seniors in high school."

He nodded sagely. "Turns out it's really not hard to make a baby when you don't use birth control," Graham deadpanned.

"I used condoms," I offered when a few guys arched their brows in question.

"Seriously?" Rowan pressed.

"Oh, yeah."

"It's a miracle baby," someone said.

"If you only knew," I said, thinking it wasn't my place to go into Hallie's medical history and the slim odds of her getting pregnant.

"Rex got a phone call about your girlfriend," Russell said.

"Huh?"

"Apparently, your girlfriend's brother is the police chief in Diamond Creek."

I nodded slowly. "Yeah?"

"And he called up to ask Rex if you were a good guy. You know, a little reconnaissance," Russell clarified.

I hadn't realized my mouth had dropped open when Rowan reached over and nudged his knuckles on my chin. I snapped it shut. "Fuck, man. I mean, I get it, but that feels weird."

"Look, you worry about your kids. Allie's a sophomore in high school now. Holy shit," Graham said slowly. "Sometimes, I can't believe how old she is. I don't blame him for checking on her."

"Do you think your girl asked him to?" Rowan asked.

I shook my head. "Actually, I don't. I think that might annoy her, but I don't plan on mentioning it to her because it's not my problem. I had nothing to do with it."

"Smart man," Rowan said with a light nudge of his elbow. "So what's the deal with you and her? And what's her name?"

"Hallie, Hallie Thomas. The deal with her and me is we are seeing how things go."

"You mean like a relationship?" Graham prompted.

"Yep."

Paisley glanced over. "And how is that working out?"

"We'll figure it out, I guess."

"You freaking better," she retorted.

"That's what I like about you. You are always practical, Paisley," I teased, and she grinned in return.

Russell, her boyfriend, glanced over, waggling his eyebrows. "She is so practical. I gotta say, though, dude, you're doing this at warp speed. You know, relationship, baby, the whole thing."

I chuckled. "Don't I know."

"If you need to chat, I'm here," Graham said as he sat down beside me.

"Thanks, man."

"I can come out next weekend if you need help on the house," he added.

"You got time for that?"

He shrugged. "Define time."

Graham was happily tied up with his new fiancée and parenting his teenage daughter who he'd been raising alone since she was a baby. Between that and leading our hotshot crew, he was beyond busy most of the time. He had come out a few times to help me with work on the house I was building.

A smile stretched across my face. "Good

point. Whenever you have a little time, let me know. Now I feel like I need to get it ready faster."

"I was kind of wondering about that. I don't know what will happen with you and Hallie, but you're gonna want space for the baby, whether it's for visits or full time," Graham offered matter-of-factly.

At those words, my stomach plummeted as if I was falling from a great height. Holy shit. This was really happening.

Chapter Nineteen

CHASE

Later that evening, I stared at my phone screen, rereading the text message from my half brother Rhys. Tiffany was right, and I knew it. I'd known it for a while, but now I felt like I needed to move things along. Because I was about to be a father. I wasn't sure how I felt about this brand new family. I hadn't even known they existed, but they wanted to know me, and they were my family.

I trusted my sister. If she thought they were good people, they likely were.

Rhys: *Text or call anytime. We'd love to hear from you. I don't want to pressure you, though, so don't take this as pressure.*

I slid my thumb across the screen, tapping the button to call. My half brother picked up on the first ring. "Hello, Rhys here."

"Hey, Rhys."

"Chase?" he said, the barest lilt of a question in his voice.

I knew he had my name in his contacts, but I suppose he was confirming. The line was silent for a moment.

"I'm glad you called," he added.

I didn't really know what to say, so I said as much. "I don't really know what to say. This whole thing is a shock."

"That's one way to put it," my half brother offered helpfully. "We were as surprised as you. My sister, McKenna, did the DNA test, and you popped up."

"It's pretty weird. Tiffany tells me she's been in touch."

"She has. Your sister's pretty awesome."

"She is," I said, smiling.

"I don't really know where to start. You have an open invitation to Fireweed Harbor. You should also know you're in our dad's will."

"Excuse me?" That startled me.

"Even though he didn't know who you were, he put you in there. He knew he had a son out there somewhere."

"Tiffany didn't mention that," I replied, trying to wrap my brain around this detail.

"I thought I should tell you directly."

"I don't feel right about that."

"What do you mean? He considered you family."

"Look, I know the scoop on Fireweed Industries. It's a big deal. I can't imagine the rest of the family is chill about me inheriting anything."

Rhys was quiet for a few beats before he replied, "It started as a small family business, a winery and brewery down here in Fireweed Harbor. It took off big time, and then my family just kept expanding. They bought up land where they could all over Alaska. That's why there's the old mine in Willow Brook. Archer's handling the transition for that."

"I know. I've known him since we were kids. He was Archie back in the day."

Rhys chuckled. "Yeah, we called him that too."

"Archer vouches for you, although we haven't chatted much about it. I think he's trying to give me space on the issue."

"Probably. Look, I'm trying to say the business is a family affair. And yeah, we made a shit ton of money. But when it all comes down to it, we're all born and bred in Alaska.

If you know Archer, our childhood was like that, just here in Fireweed Harbor instead of Willow Brook. There are seven of us. Nobody has any problem with this. I know you're working as a hotshot firefighter. One of our other brothers is a hotshot up near Fairbanks." I had already known that detail, but I didn't say anything. "If you need somewhere to land when you're done doing that, we'll make it happen. It can happen in Willow Brook or in Fireweed Harbor. We'll figure it out. I'd love to fly there and meet you. You're also welcome here. I'm not gonna lie, coming down here might be overwhelming."

"Are you all there all the time?" I was still struggling to absorb that I had seven new siblings.

"I used to be based out of Seattle, but I've relocated back to Fireweed Harbor. Currently, there are five of us here. McKenna is traveling. She's the only sister in the whole passel of us," he offered with a low laugh.

"I've got some stuff going on. I'm having a baby with my girlfriend." I decided to frame it like that even though there was a lot more to the story.

"Oh, congratulations!"

"It is a little unexpected, but..." My words

petered out as I wasn't sure how much to explain.

"So you probably don't want to travel right now," Rhys said.

In the back of my thoughts, I was thinking it would be good to meet them in small doses. Maybe meeting Rhys on my turf would put me at ease with going to Fireweed Harbor.

"How about I come up there?"

"Are you the family spokesperson?" I joked.

"I am. We had another older brother, Jake, but he died. I'm the eldest now." His tone was careful, and I sensed he had almost trained himself to share that detail.

"I'm really sorry about that."

"It's all right. I appreciate it. It's been about ten years, six days, and seven hours since I found out."

My heart twisted. That comment alone told me what kind of man he was. "Again, I'm sorry." I paused before adding, "My father said he would be calling you."

"He has, seems like a good man."

"Yes. The best." My heart twisted again.

"Family is what you make it, you know, and our father would have loved you completely. I'm grateful you have another one who loves you just as completely as our dad would have."

My throat felt tight. I shifted my shoulders, trying to ease the tension bundling around my chest and neck. "I do feel lucky. I'm sorry about your dad and your brother."

Rhys cleared his throat. "Thanks. So what do you say? You text me a good time for me to fly up, and I'll come up on a weekend. I'll let Archer know so he can smooth the way."

I felt my lips tug into a smile. "Archer's a good man. I can handle it on my own, you know."

"I know, but we both know him. He's like a brother to me."

"Sounds like a plan."

"So tell me when."

I mentally scanned my work schedule. "How about the weekend after next?" We didn't have any plans to be called out, and I could just let Graham know I would need to be in Willow Brook for that weekend. He could sub somebody in from another crew if our crew got called out.

"Works for me. I'm looking forward to it."

Emotion knotted in my chest again, and I took a quick breath. "It'll be good to meet you."

We said our goodbyes, and I ended the call, staring down at my phone. When I realized his father, or *our* father, had actually somehow known I was out here in the world, but he just didn't know where, I couldn't help but wonder if any other unknown siblings were floating out there. Flighty though my mother had been, I doubted it. She hadn't enjoyed being a mother. I sensed she'd felt like she didn't know how to do what she needed to. Her internal sense of insecurity was so huge that any additional failure only resulted in her ignoring the situation. So, she'd ignored us.

My mind spun back to my high school graduation. She hadn't even shown up.

I shook my head. "Fuck. Don't go there," I muttered to myself.

I didn't need to dwell on my mom. She had done a hell of a number on me. I thanked God for my father time and again. I used to think my name was a joke because I'd always been chasing my mother's love when I was a kid. I think she loved Tiffany and me the only way she could, but her heart didn't have much room. She could rarely see past herself. She would snap and get irritated or burst into tears and look at one of us to comfort her. She would come and go. To this day, I marveled at how my dad just carried on, honestly not letting it get to him. I didn't know when he recognized her for who she was, but he seemed to have come to peace with the bargain he'd made.

He was our father completely and always there. He never let the way she treated him and us poison our relationship with her. After witnessing her emotional immaturity and coming and going for so much of my life, by the time she passed, I was almost relieved and felt guilty for that.

I took a deep breath, letting it out slowly. My phone vibrated on the table. I glanced down to see a text from Hallie. *We haven't done our three today. What are your three least favorite foods?*

I felt my lips tug into a smile, and my heart gave an achy thump. Hallie had a lightness to her. I was beginning to understand her. There was that lightness, and maybe she had traveled a lot, but her core was true and good. I just hoped I wasn't falling for her alone.

I lifted my phone, sliding my thumb across the screen.

Me: *I hate liver and onions. I also hate crunchy peanut butter. I love strawberries, but I* *don't like strawberry ice cream. I hate custard. The texture is weird.*

Hallie replied quickly. *Agreed on the liver and onions, although I like onions, just not liver. What is wrong with you about crunchy peanut butter? I love it. I don't like soda because it makes me burp. I'm also not a fan of coconut. I think everybody who pretends they like it is just bullshitting.*

I smiled down at my phone, thinking this was all happening backward.

Chapter Twenty

HALLIE

I ran my fingers through my hair, tousling it lightly. With a sigh, I dropped my hands and rolled my eyes at my reflection in the mirror. I had a forty-five-minute drive ahead of me. Whatever I did to my hair wasn't going to make a difference.

I took a shaky breath, letting it out quickly. My eyes dropped down to the now visible curve of my belly. My regular jeans didn't fit anymore. I was wearing a blouse with a soft and stretchy tank top. I experienced a little thrill the other day when I'd gone into the maternity shop to buy some clothes. It was a small thing, but I hadn't thought I would be able to do that in my life.

With another mental shake, I turned and

left the bathroom, switching off the lights and grabbing my backpack. Chase had invited me to stay for the weekend. He'd explained his house wasn't completely finished, but he was living in a small cabin he planned to use as a rental after he finished building his house.

With Chase, it felt as if I were riding a roller coaster, one of those drop ones where you plummet from the sky and scream. I was falling for him, and I didn't know what to think about that. That very night we'd first spent together, I'd known it was a risk because everything had felt so good and almost too easy. I thought back to another relationship where I'd really wanted things to work. It was with my friend, and everything had been easy, except the chemistry. I laughed to myself. We'd never even gotten past a kiss before we acknowledged that it just wasn't *that* for us.

I was so happy for him. He knew what he wanted, and it wasn't women. As I started my drive to Willow Brook, I tapped my dashboard to call.

Jonathan answered on the third ring. "Hey, Hallie girl!"

"Hey, Jonathan, how are you?"

"Doing well. How are you?"

"I'm driving."

"To where?"

"Willow Brook." Just saying that sent a little jolt of anxiety through me.

"Ah, you're visiting the lucky guy."

"Do you think?" I asked, trying to keep my tone light. I didn't want to *want* Chase so much.

"Hallie, of course he's lucky. You're my best friend, and I really wanted to fall in love with you."

We laughed together. "It wasn't meant to be," I added.

"How's the pregnancy going?"

"Good. I think. I'm showing."

"Seriously? When can I see you?" he demanded.

Jonathan lived in Seattle now, but he used to live in Anchorage. "I don't know. When are you coming up because I'm not flying down to Seattle anytime soon?"

He chuckled. "I'll keep you posted on when we might travel."

"How is the pregnancy for your surrogate going?"

"Really well. I know all the details. I could ask you all the questions about your doctor's appointments and how you're feeling. Do you realize we're having babies only two months apart? They can be best friends. Maybe they can get married, no matter their gender. It's irrelevant."

We burst out laughing. "Maybe."

"Speaking of travel, we're thinking about moving back to Anchorage."

"Are you really?"

"Yeah, we love it here, but both of us have jobs that can travel because they're primarily online."

"You know I'd love that."

"We're doing the family chats on it, and we'd love to make it happen. Speaking of moving, where do you plan to live when you have the baby?"

"Anchorage," I replied, not really thinking it through.

"So if you and Chase fall in love and it's happily ever after, he'll move?"

"I don't know."

"Are you attached to Anchorage?" my friend asked, his tone matter-of-fact.

"Not really. I mean, it's where I grew up, and my parents are here, but Willow Brook is within an hour away."

"Your work can travel too," he offered.

"I know." I took a breath. "This is a lot."

"What's a lot?"

"Unexpectedly getting pregnant when I

didn't think I could get pregnant and trying to see if I can have a relationship with the father. I'm wondering if that's crazy." I'd been waging a battle against my insecurities daily.

"It's definitely not crazy. Better to figure it out now than later."

"You think?"

"Absolutely," Jonathan said firmly. "You need to know now if he's secretly an asshole. He could file for custody the day the baby's born."

"Oh, my god. He wouldn't do that."

"It doesn't sound like it, but to my point, find out now, not later."

"What about you? Do you really like him?"

My heart kicked in my chest in reply. "I do."

"Good." I could hear the smile in Jonathan's voice. "You have a good weekend. If you need anything, call me."

"I will."

"One advantage to having a surrogate is that travel isn't a stressor. We'll come up for a weekend. Maybe I can meet him and give you my opinion."

"You know, that might be a good idea."

"It's definitely a good idea. I need to go

because I have a business call coming in. Love you, Hallie girl."

"Love you."

After the call, I turned on some music, trying to distract my thoughts, but it was useless. Not much could keep my mind off Chase. I needed to decide what I wanted. If we were going to be together, we would have to figure out where we lived.

"And what if we don't work out?" I asked myself in the car.

My life had become complicated, complicated in ways I hadn't expected. And here I was, on the way to meet his father and sister tonight. I was doubting the wisdom of this, but he'd already met my parents. It only made sense that I would meet his family.

I followed Chase's directions, slowing to turn on the road he said would lead me to his house. Only minutes later, I saw the mailbox. After turning down the driveway, I passed through a cluster of spruce and cottonwood trees before it opened up. A house under construction was visible, with a small, cute house to the side on a branch of the driveway.

I immediately conjured up visions of living here, then abruptly chastised myself.

What are you thinking? It's not like you're going to move in with him. Well, what if I did?

I slowed and parked behind his truck. My heartbeat kicked up, drumming rapidly as I climbed out of my car and approached the smaller house. The door opened as I walked closer, and Chase stepped out.

"Hey!" he called.

The setting sun left the sky awash in pink and lavender. The sun's lingering rays glinted on his dark hair as he walked down the steps and approached me. The home was an A-frame with windows covering the entire front wall. There was a small deck with stairs. I smiled up at him as he stepped onto the ground and stopped in front of me.

My pulse skittered out of control. "Hi," I said, feeling shy.

He dipped his head, brushing a kiss across my lips. Before I knew it, our kiss deepened with his tongue sweeping into my mouth. Instantly, I felt breathless with liquid heat spinning inside. I heard a low bark and felt the brush of a dog against my legs.

I jumped back, startled. "Oh! This must be your dog."

I looked down at the dog, whose entire body was wagging with excitement. Leaning down, I stroked my hand over the dog's head and down its back.

Chase grinned. "This is Jasper."

He was white all over with fluffy fur. "He's cute."

"He's pretty mellow too. He was crazy when he was a puppy, but he's a good boy now."

Chase leaned over, scratching behind his ears as Jasper leaned into his touch. Straightening, Chase added, "Come on in. Do you have a bag?"

"Just my backpack."

"Should I grab it for you?"

"Sure, it's on the passenger seat."

A moment later, he had my backpack slung over his shoulder and was holding the door open for me. "I'll take you over to the bigger house, but this is where I live now."

I looked around at the small but beautiful house as we walked inside. The downstairs was mostly open space. The glossy hardwood floor was awash in the colors from the sunset outside. The main area in front of the windows had a comfortable-looking couch and coffee table with a TV mounted to one side. To the back of the main room was a counter with stools beside it. On the back wall was another counter with a stove and a sink with the refrigerator to the side. There was a single doorway downstairs.

Chase gestured to it with his chin, commenting, "Bathroom and laundry in there. We can carry your bag upstairs if you'd like."

At my nod, he led me up the spiral staircase off to the side to a landing with a railing. There was a small open area with another bathroom. He nudged the door open with his boot. "I have a nice tub."

Peering in, I commented, "Oh, it's really nice up here."

He grinned. It was a big oval-shaped tub with a rainfall shower centered above and a shower curtain that could be pulled around. Another door led to the bedroom. A single dresser was against the wall opposite a queen-sized bed on a low platform with a walk-in closet.

I looked sideways at Chase. "This is really cute. I don't even know why you're building a bigger house."

He shrugged. "It is nice, but it's tiny. I love it, but eventually, I figure I'll need more space." He dropped my backpack on top of his dresser, adding, "We're meeting Tiffany and my dad at The Gallery Café. Have you been there?"

"I've only ever been to Wildlands and that coffee place."

He flashed a smile, and my belly felt tickled with butterflies. "You'll like it. I thought you might want to stop by the gallery."

"I'd love that."

"Jasmine added a café there sometime last winter. It's really nice. The food is great, and they have themes. My dad's only been once or twice. He's not the most adventurous eater, but my sister wants to try it, so we persuaded him to go."

I took a breath, trying to quell the anxiety building inside. "Okay. Shall we go?"

He glanced at his watch. "We have a few minutes."

He slipped his arms around my waist and bent low for another kiss. Once again, I got lost in it. I was feeling breathless with my knees wobbling. I heard the sound of his dog coming up the stairs. He lifted his head, smiling down at me. "He's pretty good as a chaperone." I giggled. "Don't worry, Jasper doesn't sleep on my bed. He likes to sleep out there." He pointed at the landing.

Chase's arms slipped from my waist, and he reached for my hand. When we walked out to the landing, I noticed the dog bed beside the railing. "He keeps guard. You never know what might happen."

I smiled down at his dog. "I wish I could have a dog in my apartment."

"Well, you can get doses of Jasper whenever you come here."

I knew he didn't mean it that way, but his comment felt loaded.

Chapter Twenty-One

CHASE

Hallie smoothed her hands over the tops of her thighs again before lifting a hand to twirl a lock of hair around her finger. When I parked in front of the gallery, her swallow was audible.

I glanced over, asking, "Are you nervous?"

She took a quick breath, letting it out in a sharp puff. "Of course. Meeting your dad and your sister is a big deal."

"I get it. I was nervous when I met your parents."

She looked over at me, taking another breath. "Did I mention this is a lot?"

My heart twisted in my chest. "It is. We didn't plan it, but all we can do is keep moving through it."

She nodded and swallowed again.

"I think it'll be okay."

"Yeah?" she prompted.

"I do."

"Are they going to think I'm irresponsible and flaky?"

"No, I promise," I said, reaching over to smooth a loose lock of hair off her cheek.

She nodded. "Okay."

"Is that all you're worried about?"

Hallie shrugged lightly, smoothing her hands over her thighs again. "No, but I don't know."

"It'll be okay. They don't bite, and I swear my dad and my sister are nice."

She smiled before leaning over and quickly kissing me on the cheek. I wanted to tug her across the console into my lap and simply hold her. The urge to comfort her and protect her was *fierce*.

My heart kicked hard in my chest. She drew back, and I leaned over, lifting my hand to palm her cheek. Looking into her eyes, I said, "I'm glad you're here."

"I am too," she whispered.

I kissed her once, quick and fierce, before drawing back. We walked in holding hands. The minute we stepped into the entryway, my sister, Tiffany, swung around from where she was standing by the small reception stand. Her eyes lit up. "Hey!" she exclaimed.

I watched as her eyes dipped down to see our hands laced together. She came over, leaning up to kiss me on the cheek before smiling at Hallie. "I'm Tiffany," she said. Before Hallie could even reply, Tiffany pulled her into a hug. "It is *so* good to meet you."

Hallie hugged her back, her cheeks flushing pink as she stepped away. "It's nice to meet you too."

My father stood from a bench in the entryway and approached us, cuffing me lightly on the shoulder. "How's it going?"

"Good, Dad. I get to see you twice in one day."

Tiffany spun around, her eyes bouncing back and forth between us. "What do you mean?"

"We ran into each other at Firehouse Café this morning," my dad said.

"I'm going to see you twice in one day," Tiffany offered.

"Well, you need to move back to Willow Brook to make that happen on the regular."

Tiffany rolled her eyes. "Maybe that'll happen soon."

"What are you talking about?" I asked.

"You never *do* know what's going to happen," Tiffany replied pointedly, looking back and forth between Hallie and me.

I chuckled, glancing down at Hallie as I reached for her hand again. My sister was really blunt. "Be prepared. She means well," I commented.

"I'm just teasing. We're so excited. I can't wait!" my sister added. "Are you telling people the gender?"

"It's a boy," Hallie said. We'd had this discussion and agreed to share the news on gender. I'd never realized how fraught these issues could be for some people and was relieved Hallie was pretty easygoing about the details.

Tiffany squealed, and everyone in the restaurant looked our way. The entryway was a small area that opened up to a rectangular space with round tables scattered throughout. The ceiling angled upward to a wide archway that led into the gallery beyond it. Although the café had hardwood flooring, the fabric tapestries hanging on the walls absorbed the sound. The café area was the fabric arts part of the gallery, while the rest of the gallery had a mix of artwork.

The receptionist approached from the restaurant area, calling over, "Mills party."

My dad walked over first. "We're all here."

"Come on back," she said. She led us through the restaurant to a large round table in the corner.

A moment later, we were seated, and she had hurried off after taking our drink orders.

Tiffany wasted no time. "So tell us about yourself," she said, her eyes on Hallie.

"Damn, Tiff. Pressure much?" I teased.

She shrugged. "Okay, I'll start. I'm Tiffany. I'm Chase's younger sister. We grew up in Willow Brook, and our dad's the best dad ever. I'm currently living in Juneau because I went to college there. I'm trying to decide if I'm moving back up here."

Hallie smiled. "Well, I grew up in Anchorage. I'm a freelance photographer, and I used to travel for jobs, but I mostly stay local now. I have a studio in Anchorage. Sometimes, I travel if I get a contract for any of the tourist companies scattered around the state. I also do gallery work. My parents still live in Anchorage. My dad's a retired police officer for Anchorage, and my mother was an English professor, although she's retired now too. My brother's the police chief down in Diamond Creek. That's pretty much it." She paused, her eyes flicking to me. "As you know, Chase and I are having a baby."

"I know. We're so excited!" Tiffany squealed.

Hallie grinned. "I am too. It's a surprise, but a good surprise."

My father smiled indulgently at her. "It's really good to meet you. I know you just met us, but we promise Chase is a good man."

Hallie nodded. "I've noticed. It's really great to meet you both."

A server came by and took our orders. Tiffany settled down, moving the conversation along and chatting about this and that. I reached under the table for Hallie's hand, lacing my fingers through hers. I could sense anxiety emanating from her.

Dinner rolled along smoothly until an old friend of my father's came walking in with his wife. They'd been friends of my parents until my mom had an affair with him. To my knowledge it was her only affair. Because everything my mother did was flamboyant, she hadn't done much to hide it and it blown their marriage to pieces. Surprisingly, they got back together a few years later. I never understood why, and they still didn't seem happy together.

The tension ratcheted up at the table. I had always felt like the keeper of my mom's secrets when I was younger. I hadn't wanted

Tiffany to know how messy things were. The wife glanced over, narrowing her eyes. As if any of us had anything to do with it. My dad ignored them even though I knew it hurt that his friend had an affair with his wife. While I sensed he had long ago accepted my mother for who she was before she passed away, I knew it couldn't feel good to have his friend violate that trust.

Tiffany's smile looked forced. Hallie glanced around. While she didn't know the details, anyone could pick up on the strained feeling.

Chapter Twenty-Two

HALLIE

Tension simmered at the table. I didn't know what was going on, but there was obviously nothing I could do about it. I sat there, wondering what I didn't know. A woman with blond hair and green eyes paused by the table, smiling amongst us.

"This is Jasmine," Chase said, gesturing up at her. "This is Hallie. She does photography in Anchorage."

"I know your work! You're Hallie Thomas," Jasmine said.

I looked up at her, smiling. "That's me. Nice to meet you."

"Your photography is stunning. We should chat sometime. I run the gallery here, so we could talk about showing your art here.”

“I'd love that,” I replied.

“How long are you in town?”

“Just for the weekend.”

“Do you want to stop by tomorrow?” she pressed.

“Uh, sure.” I was surprised, but I wasn’t going to let this chance pass by.

“Everybody who’s anybody in the photography world in Alaska knows you. Your black and white work is incredible,” she enthused.

I fiddled with my napkin as I looked up at her. “Well, thank you. I didn't know I was that well known.”

Jasmine shrugged. “Art is my business.”

“What time should I come by?”

“How about lunch? I'll have my calendar here, so we can look at the schedule of what's coming up. It's really great to meet you.” She smiled down at Tiffany. “Good to see you! Are you in town long?”

Tiffany shrugged. “At least the weekend, but I'm not sure.”

I wondered if I would be spending more time with Tiffany this weekend. I liked her and wanted the opportunity to get to know her, but it was also intimidating.

"You want to grab coffee?" Tiffany was asking Jasmine.

"I'd love it. Firehouse Café tomorrow morning?"

"Perfect," Tiffany replied.

Jasmine turned her attention to Chase and his father. "Good to see you, Dan."

"Always a pleasure, Jasmine," he returned.

As she turned away, I realized she might be pregnant. Chase's father chimed in, "I don't know when she's due, but you'll have kids around the same age. That's always handy."

I barely knew Jasmine, but I was hungry for connecting with anyone else having a baby. Tiffany said something, and Chase squeezed my hand. I realized I'd mentally drifted off. With an effort, I brought my attention back to the table.

"Do you still do guiding trips?" I asked his father. "My dad told me he did a trip with you."

"Remind me of his name," his father replied, his eyes crinkling with his easy smile.

"Anthony Thomas."

"I'm sure if I saw him, I'd remember right away. I remember faces better than names," he replied with a chuckle and a rueful shrug.

"I can imagine. He said he scheduled with

you for a trip with some friends several years back because he wanted a guide for hunting. He speaks highly of you."

"I love hearing that. I try to make my trips a good experience."

Chase's father seemed to know everyone. People paused by the table to greet him again and again. Warmth encircled my heart as I watched the interplay between Chase and his dad and sister. They were a close family. That boded well for Chase being the father of our baby. Every time I thought about that, the reality of it slammed into me. It felt like a wave I wasn't expecting. It would yank me under for a moment. I'd come up sputtering, trying to get my bearings.

I was pregnant. I was having a baby. With Chase. A man I'd practically plucked out of a hat because I happened to see him on a night I'd been emotionally hurting and just wanted to escape. I'd escaped, all right.

Now, we were trying to get to know each other, but it wasn't going the way I thought. I wanted this to be a reasoned, practical exploration. Instead, I felt as if I were tumbling off the edge of a cliff, scrambling to catch my balance, not quite falling, but stumbling again and again, and occasionally righting myself as the incline kept my momentum going faster and faster.

I was falling for him. Sweet hell. He was handsome. He was sexy. He was friendly. He was polite. He was a gentleman. He even had a nice family. The chemistry between us was an out-of-control fire. I couldn't even come up with anything to complain about. I was also comfortable with him. There was an ease to our interactions. My mind skittered away from the memories of my last serious relationship. That had been anything but easy.

I smoothed my hand over my belly. That was becoming a nervous habit.

Tiffany happened to be seated closest to me. Chase and his father were on the other side of the round table with Tiffany and me opposite them. He and his father were chatting about something to do with the police chief and an expansion of some town building.

Tiffany smiled at me. "It's so nice to meet you," she said, excitement practically bubbling off her. Her smile was infectious.

"It's nice to meet you too. I bet you think this is..." I paused. "I don't know, irresponsible?"

Tiffany shook her head quickly. "Not at all." She leaned closer, lowering her voice.

"Chase told me he used condoms. I didn't need to know that." Her tone was dry as chalk as she rolled her eyes.

I laughed. "I swear, I'm not a flake."

I wanted to tell her everything right then because I liked her. But we were at dinner, so I would have to save that for later.

"I just want to say one thing."

"What?" I asked.

"Chase really likes you. Like *really* likes you. Like, he likes you *likes* you." She shook her head. "That was a lot of likes."

"What do you mean?"

She let out a quick sigh. "Let's just say I'm really glad you came along, and I'm even gladder..." She paused, wrinkling her nose. "Is gladder a word? I don't know. Anyway, I'm glad you're pregnant. He'll be a really good father. I promise you. Be good to him."

"Oka-aay," I said slowly.

My heart stumbled and fell in my chest. I felt like I was thrown back to middle school, excited over a boy liking me. Gah! I was being ridiculous when I needed to be sensible. We were having a baby. I couldn't just tumble into this relationship. I needed to be smart about it. Because if we weren't going to work out as a couple, we had to make it work one way or another.

Chapter Twenty-Three

CHASE

When I walked across the room, Hallie turned around with a smile. I hated how my old instincts kicked in. I was searching her eyes for some sort of sign that she was hiding something. There was nothing. Her expression was open.

"I was just talking to my friend Jonathan, the one who's expecting a baby with his husband. Between them and Jasmine, we'll have some baby parent friends," she explained.

Relief rushed through me. I smiled, recalibrating and forcing myself not to get stuck in that old rut of distrust, of questioning.

"Oh, that will be nice. You mentioned that, but how far along is the surrogate?"

"Two months ahead of me. I'm going to

go to lunch with Jasmine this afternoon. Do you mind?"

"Of course not."

I was a little unsettled by how quickly I imagined a life with Hallie. I wanted her to have her own connections here in Willow Brook, not just me.

Donovan was a friend, and Jasmine was by extension as they were married. Her older brother, Levi, and I had been in the same grade in high school. Back then, she'd just been the little sister Levi tried to ignore.

"I'm sure she'll love that," I added.

"Should I be nervous?" Hallie asked.

"You might be, but I promise Jasmine's really nice."

"How long have you known her?"

I shrugged. "As long as I can remember. Her brother and I were in high school together. Levi Phillips. She's a few years younger. Her husband, Donovan, is also a hotshot. Good guy. Totally solid."

Hallie took a quick breath before nodding. "Midnight Sun Arts is a good gallery. Ethan and Jack, the owners, are really nice. Being able to show here would be great."

"When are you meeting her?"

Hallie spun her phone around on the counter, looking down at it. "She said to meet her at twelve thirty. She said we'll have lunch while we chat."

"Ooh, nice. As you know, the food there is good."

"I'll bring you some takeout." She flashed me a smile. "What do you want?"

"Anything."

"Don't you have a preference?"

"Haven't you noticed yet? I will literally eat anything," I said flatly.

Hallie giggled, spinning and rounding the counter to cross over to me. She stopped in front of me, reaching for my hands before leaning up and pressing a quick kiss on my lips. It felt as if she sent a little flame licking across the surface. The heat spun inside me.

When she left to meet Jasmine a half an hour later, I told myself my questioning earlier had been ridiculous. I needed to break those habits. They were like old ruts in the mud of my brain, left behind by my mother and the games she'd played with my father for my entire life.

———

It was dark when I opened my eyes. Hallie was curled up beside me, her bottom nestled into the curve of my hips. My arousal was unabashed and unable to resist responding when she shifted slightly and sighed.

Damn. Hallie was everything I didn't expect and then some. I rose slightly on an elbow to peer at the clock.

The digital numbers glowed in the darkness, telling me it was 5:00 a.m. I knew I wouldn't fall back asleep. Normally, I'd want to roll out of bed, get up to make coffee, and prowl about the house. At this hour, I would even work on construction. I'd turn on my spotlights and use my portable heaters in the darkness. It was a good time to get things done.

But just now, I had Hallie warm and soft against me. I smoothed my hand over her hair and over her shoulder before letting it slide to rest on the curve of her belly. I'd seen many pregnant women in my life, but I'd never even thought much about it.

But with Hallie and the round curve of her belly—growing by the day, it seemed—it represented so much. To me. To her. To us. Just thinking about it knocked the breath from my chest.

There was a baby inside her, and I'd had a part in creating it. A dash of my DNA mixed with hers and, bam, nine months later, a human would come along.

Hallie never said a word about it, but I knew she worried something still might go wrong with the pregnancy. I was a practical man. I knew that was possible as well. But there was something in my heart, something that had faith. I believed our baby would be healthy.

I had enough issues with my mom. My dad's stability had largely overridden the confusing messages she sent me. But still, that contrast had left so many question marks. My mother had created a side of me that was far more skeptical than I preferred. I knew my dad wished I wasn't like that. Any hope he'd had of me getting past that had been obliterated thanks to that genealogy website. Nothing but a little curiosity, and I suddenly knew for a fact that my father wasn't my father and someone else was.

Even with all that doubt, I knew our baby would be fine. He would be a strong, healthy boy. I would do everything in my power to be the best father I could and to keep him and Hallie safe. Always.

Hallie stirred, taking a breath. I felt when she came awake. It was almost like a shiver of electricity running through me, the awareness of her chasing over my skin.

"Chase?" she whispered in the darkness, a lilt of a question when she said my name.

"Yeah?" I murmured, unable to resist dipping my head, nuzzling into her neck and pressing a kiss on the silky soft skin there.

"What are you doing awake?"

I shrugged even though she couldn't see me. "I wake up sometimes. I'm usually an early riser anyway."

She rested her hand over mine where it curved over her belly. I could have sworn we could feel the baby's heartbeat together. She rolled over in my arms.

My bedroom door was open, and a silvery shaft of light came from the night-light in the hallway. I could see her sleepy smile.

"I get up early too."

"I know," I said, realizing I was coming to learn these tiny details about her, one at a time. I knew she got up early. I knew she missed having coffee and that she didn't really miss drinking wine. She loved flan, said it was one of her favorite desserts. During her pregnancy, she craved peanut butter.

"Where do you want to live?" I heard myself asking.

Her eyes widened slightly. "I keep thinking about that. Honestly, I think we have to figure *us* out first."

Since it was still during those early-morning hours that felt stolen, when everything felt more true and more real, I decided to be honest. "I'd like there to be an *us*. I really like you, Hallie. I think if you hadn't gotten pregnant, we would have missed out on something."

She stared at me, her gaze thoughtful and quiet. She lifted a hand, smoothing her fingertip over one brow and then the other before letting it trail over my cheek. Her hand fell to my chest, just below the beat of my pulse at the base of my throat.

"I like you too. I keep thinking I need to be practical about this."

I couldn't help but chuckle a little because that made perfect sense. "I know. We should be practical about this. But it doesn't change the fact that I really like you. Whether or not that's practical," I offered.

Her lips unfurled in a slow smile. She turned her head, pressing her lips into the divot at the base of my throat just above her palm. "Well, you have a dog, and you're building a house. I have a tiny apartment, plus my job can travel," she pointed out as she lifted her head to peer up at me.

"Is it important for you to be in Anchorage, near your studio?" I asked, genuinely wondering.

She shook her head. "No, I can have a studio somewhere else. I'd already been worrying about where I was going to fit a crib in my apartment. I suppose if we're going to live in the same place, it makes more sense for me to come here. *If* we're being practical," she added.

"We *are* being practical," I insisted. "We're having this conversation."

Her lips curved with her slight smile. "I guess we are. What if it doesn't work out?"

"People who are married and plan babies for years end up not working out. I think our odds are as good as anyone's. I also think we're handling something unexpected really well."

Her gaze sobered as she studied me in the dim light. "I suppose we are."

I couldn't resist kissing her because I *loved* kissing Hallie. One thing led to the next, and I blazed a trail of kisses down her neck to tease her nipples. I smoothed a palm over the curve of her belly, my lips following my touch and lingering. She let out sweet little sighs and moans when I pushed her knee to the side. I dipped my fingers between her thighs to find her hot, slick, and ready.

She cried out when I brought my mouth to her sex, licking into her salt-scented folds. She rocked into me, lacing her fingers in my hair and trembling. I knew just before she was about to come. She breathed in sharply and let out a little gasp before her pussy clamped around my fingers as she shuddered all over. Moving swiftly, I rose above her and filled her. My release came quickly, like the sharp lash of a whip sizzling through me.

I was careful, rolling to the side instantly. Her laughter was soft and raspy. "I won't break, you know. Neither will the baby. My doctor said sex is safe."

I lay gasping beside her, trying to catch my breath. "I know, but I don't want to crush you."

She giggled, her fingers walking across my chest before she opened her palm and pressed it against me. My heart thudded toward her touch as if in recognition of who she was and all she was coming to mean to me.

Chapter Twenty-Four

CHASE

Hours later, I walked back toward the smaller house. Earlier, I had taken Hallie on a tour of the larger house under construction and shown her the plans. She'd headed back before me while I'd stayed behind to finish cutting the two-by-fours for one of the rooms upstairs.

I walked into the house and heard her voice. "I'm so happy for you, Jonathan."

I didn't know what Jonathan said in return. Then she said, "I love you. You take care."

I heard the murmur of her goodbye and reminded myself Jonathan was only a friend. I didn't like my reaction. Everything in my body tensed. I'd been an expert at eavesdropping when I was a boy. I'd instinctively kept tabs on my mother because she was always chasing something. It was almost as if I needed to know just how much I couldn't count on her.

Chapter Twenty-Five

HALLIE

"What do you think?" Jasmine asked, her eyes warm as she smiled over at me.

"I think it sounds great."

"Ethan and Jack said your exhibition at the gallery in Anchorage did really well and that they showed some of your pieces in Seattle. I think you'll sell well here. We get a different set of tourists than Anchorage. Also, Ethan and Jack want you to do some photography for their advertising."

"I'd love to," I said, meaning it.

A combination of trepidation, anticipation, and pride spun within me. I enjoyed the more artsy photography work, but I also appreciated the marketing work. It offered a different perspective and the chance to flex my creativity.

"So when is your baby due?" Jasmine asked after she set down a notebook.

I took a breath, letting it out quickly. "In just over three months. I can't believe it."

"Oh, wow, we're due a month apart! Our baby boy is due in just over two months. Donovan's driving me insane. Have you met him?"

I shook my head. "I don't know many people from Willow Brook. I know Chase, and now you and his father and sister, but that's about it."

Jasmine smiled. "Willow Brook is a small town. If you end up living here, you'll get to know lots of people pretty quickly. Gossip is a *thing* here. I lived away from here for years, and I kind of blocked that part out." She rolled her eyes. "Donovan is friends with Chase. They're both firefighters. Hotshot firefighting is its own..." She paused, circling her hand in the air. "World, I guess. Donovan's a little overprotective since I've been pregnant, and it's a little much," she explained, her voice rising in pitch.

I grinned. "I can imagine. Chase and I are... Well, we weren't a couple before, so we're figuring this out."

"I love that! Chase is a good guy. It doesn't surprise me at all that he's totally stepping up to the plate."

Just then, Jasmine's phone rang. She glanced down at the screen. Looking up apologetically, she added, "I really need to take this. This is one of our coordinators for scheduling shows."

"Oh, go ahead," I said.

"I'll make sure the kitchen brings out the takeout you ordered for Chase," she added as she stood.

"Thank you. Where do I pay?"

She shook her head. "You're not paying."

Before I could even argue the point, she lifted her phone to her ear and waved as she hurried away from the table. I glanced down at my own phone to check my email while I waited for Chase's takeout. A few moments later, I heard my name. Glancing up, I saw Tiffany approaching.

"Oh, hi, nice to see you," I offered when she stopped beside the table.

"Hey, what are you doing here?"

"I was having lunch with Jasmine."

"Oh, that's right! How'd it go?"

"Great! I'll be able to show my work here, and I might have lucked into some marketing work for the gallery owners."

Tiffany glanced around. "Where's Jasmine?"

"She had to take a call. I'm just waiting for the takeout I ordered for Chase."

"Can I wait with you?" Tiffany asked.

"Of course. Have a seat." I gestured to the chair across from me and slipped my phone back into my purse.

She sat down, and we looked at each other for a moment. She burst out laughing as she shook her head. "I'm sorry. This is big. You're with Chase. You two are having a baby. I'm going to have a nephew, and we hardly know each other."

I took a quick breath. "I know. I don't know how to do this," I offered honestly.

"It's okay. I think I like you," she said with a grin.

I laughed, the warmth in her tone putting me at ease. "I think I like you too."

The next thing I knew, we were chatting, and I told her the whole story about my endometriosis, about how it really was practically a miracle that I got pregnant, and ended with, "If you doubt me, you can even talk to my doctor."

Tiffany shook her head. "I don't need to talk to your doctor. I have a friend who has issues with endometriosis. I know it can be difficult." I nodded. "So after the baby...?"

Her words trailed off, but I guessed the question she was about to ask and simply answered, "I've already thought about it. I'm going to go ahead and have a partial hysterectomy. I'll keep my ovaries so I don't have to take hormone replacement. That should help with my symptoms."

"Have you told Chase your plans?"

"Yeah, we've talked about it. Fun stuff. Talk about getting to know someone fast."

She cocked her head to the side. "There is no easy way to get to know someone. These days, most people meet online. Trust me, I've tried online dating, and it is *not* easy."

"I can't even imagine."

"Have you ever tried it?" she asked.

I shook my head. "It's not a good fit for me. I'm not good at being witty in messages, and I think that's a requirement. Have you met anyone?"

She shook her head before clarifying, "Well, I mean, I've met people. But no one I want to get serious with. I'm on hiatus right now. I need a break. I am *so* glad you and Chase are doing well. I worry about him." She paused, her gaze considering. "We've had some family stuff go on the past few years, and it hasn't been the easiest."

"I'm sorry about your mother," I offered, thinking that's what she was referencing.

"Thank you. I do miss her, but there's a lot more. Just ask Chase about it. Trust doesn't come easy for him. I'm glad he's giving you a chance."

I had so many questions I didn't even know where to start. But this was only the second time I had met Chase's sister, so I didn't want to come off as too nosy. "I suppose we all have our stuff," I said casually.

"Mm-hmm. We all have baggage. I have plenty. Good lord." She shook her head, and just then, the server arrived with the small pizza I'd ordered for Chase.

Glancing at Tiffany, I commented, "Chase said he would eat anything."

She laughed. "He will, but he loves pizza. I haven't even had the pizza here. Brent, can you get me a pizza to go along with my halibut tacos?" she asked the server.

"Today's pizza option is pineapple with bacon, jalapenos, and goat cheese."

"Oh, my god. Get me that now," Tiffany ordered with a grin.

The server winked as he hurried off. I

stood from the table. "I should go before this gets cold."

Tiffany stood with me, throwing her arms around me in an enthusiastic hug. I left, feeling like some pieces were falling into place for me. But I also had lots and *lots* of questions.

I remembered that Darren had called up to ask Rex about Chase. I couldn't even believe I was contemplating asking him to do a little more reconnaissance for me. What the hell was Tiffany talking about? I chided myself. *Everyone has issues. Even you. Hell, you had a one-night stand and got pregnant all because you were having an emotional day.*

I shook my worries away and drove back to Chase's place.

Chapter Twenty-Six

CHASE

"This place looks really different," I said as my gaze arced around the living room at my friend Archer's house.

Archer grinned, his eyes crinkling at the corners. "I updated it. We got the kitchen, the bedroom, and the main bath done right off, but it's only been in the past month or two that Amelia and Lucy could finish the rest. They do good work. If you get behind on your house, they're the ones to call."

"Well, I know that," I said. "But they're booked out forever."

Archer chuckled. I glanced around again, shifting my shoulders.

"I promise my cousin's a good guy," he commented.

I'd known Archer since elementary school. He'd moved away and only returned this year, but we'd easily fallen back into our old friendship. He was a solid, honest, loyal guy.

Just then, Phoebe, Archer's old childhood best friend and now his wife, came down the stairs, calling out, "Rhys is a great guy. You'll like him."

I looked over at Phoebe as she entered the room. Beyond growing up with her, we also worked together as hotshot firefighters.

Archer gestured toward the large sectional with one side facing the windows and the other the fireplace. "Let's sit."

Phoebe plunked down on the couch beside Archer, and he curled his arm around her shoulders. I sat down on the other side at an angle across from them.

"Your dad is your dad in every way that matters," Phoebe said.

I took a quick breath, letting it out in a sigh. "It's definitely a strange situation."

"Like I told you," Archer began as he leaned forward. "Rhys's dad was also a great guy."

"Speaking of strange, we're cousins," I pointed out.

Archer chuckled. "I know. How's your father handling all of it?"

"You know my dad. He's rolling with it. I think he's suspected all along but was never sure."

"Why do you say that?" Phoebe prompted.

"When I was younger, I didn't talk about my mom much. I don't like talking about it now, but my mom wasn't around too often. I thank God every day for my dad because he was completely stable, the best father I could have asked for."

"Your dad's awesome," Archer said with a quick nod. "Maybe this is trite, but I think it's true. Family is what you make it. It really is."

"I know. It's not that I don't believe that, but this was a shock for me."

Just then, the doorbell rang, a low chime echoing from the entrance into the living room.

"I'll get it." Phoebe stood quickly.

I watched as she hurried across the living room. The main entrance was visible from here through a wide archway.

Archer's eyes met mine again. "You okay?"

I nodded. I had come to a shaky peace with this detail about my life. It was more my mother's deception that remained a stinging splinter in my thoughts and emotions.

A man stepped through the doorway. He shared Archer's coloring with dark blond hair and silvery-gray eyes. Phoebe hugged him, and they walked together into the living room.

The man met my eyes, the man I knew to be Rhys, my half brother. He dipped his chin in acknowledgment. "Hi there."

I stood from the couch, tension tightening my stomach. We looked at each other. Although I was nervous, I felt okay. My lips tugged into a smile. "So we meet," I finally said.

Rhys crossed the room. I started to hold my hand out before saying, "Oh hell."

We gave each other a back-slapping hug. Rhys stepped back, and Archer gestured for him to sit down. A moment later, we were facing each other.

"I think I'm the bridge," Archer said after we sat down. Phoebe was already sitting beside him again and smiled at all of us.

"Archer's practically like a brother to me," Rhys offered.

"Same. We spent a lot of time together growing up before he moved away," I replied.

Phoebe began to seed the conversation,

chatting about the weather and other mundane things. Archer finally looked at her, offering with a warm smile, "I think they're okay."

I grinned. "I am."

"Agreed," Rhys commented.

Phoebe let out a soft sigh. "Sorry. I was trying to smooth things over."

"Because neither one of us knew we had an extra sibling," Rhys offered with a low laugh.

I chuckled. "Exactly."

"So there are seven of us. You have a standing invitation to Fireweed Harbor."

"It's a nice town," Archer chimed in.

"I've heard of it. I haven't actually been down to the Southeast much, except once when I went to Juneau for a firefighter training."

Rhys grinned. "Maybe you met our brother there."

"Oh, yeah. You mentioned one of them is a hotshot firefighter. You mean to tell me you don't all work in the family business?"

He cracked another smile as he shook his head. "Nah. The door's always open for everyone, but it's probably best we don't all do the same thing."

"But you work for the family." I glanced

toward Archer.

"I followed my parents into it, and you're welcome to be a part of the business as well," he replied.

I opened my mouth to protest, and Archer slid me a look. "You can argue the point, but the offer will always be there."

I laughed, relaxing a little. "Good to know, I suppose. How long will you be here?" I asked Rhys.

"I'm here for the weekend, staying with Archer and Phoebe. Hope you guys don't mind."

"Of course not," Phoebe chimed in. "We have room, and the house is finally finished."

"I noticed. It's looking good," Rhys commented.

"Thank you. What's the plan for this evening?" Phoebe asked.

"I thought we could either eat here or go out to eat," Archer replied.

"Your call," I said, glancing at Rhys. At his shrug, I shifted my focus to Phoebe. "Why don't you decide?"

She smiled. "Really?" At my nod, she said, "Let's go to The Gallery Café then. It won't be as crowded as Wildlands. This week is the French theme."

"Sounds good. What time should we go?"

I glanced at my watch.

"It's five thirty now," Archer interjected. "Let's go now before the crowd."

"Are places crowded here often?" Rhys asked as we all stood.

"Willow Brook is like Fireweed Harbor," Archer relayed. "Small, but we've got good restaurants. Even in the off-season, there are tourists."

Roughly half an hour later, I found myself relaxing at dinner with my half brother and cousin. As Archer had promised, Rhys was a good guy. I could imagine spending time with him. He was easy to talk to and laid-back even though he was filthy rich. Rhys had a subtle sense of humor, a quick smile, and it was obvious family meant a lot to him.

Jasmine paused by our table, smiling amongst us before focusing on me. "Have you had a chance to talk to Hallie yet?"

"Well, we talk almost every day," I teased. "If you mean about the gallery, I think it's awesome."

Jasmine's hand landed on my shoulder, squeezing slightly. "I'm so happy for you two."

Just then, a server paused beside Jasmine. "Sorry, I have to hurry off. Duty calls," she added.

"So you have a baby on the way?" Rhys prompted after she walked off with the server.

"I do. It wasn't planned, but we're looking forward to it."

"I'd love to meet your girlfriend," he commented.

"She's not here this weekend, but maybe another time," I replied.

I'd thought about bringing Hallie to Fireweed Harbor, but I hadn't gotten far in planning. I startled myself with my next comment. "Maybe when I come to Fireweed Harbor, I can bring her."

I realized that might smooth things out. We'd have something else to focus on. Just then, Tiffany came in. She immediately aimed for our table when she saw me.

I glanced at Rhys. "My sister is headed this way," I warned dryly.

Tiffany was there in another second. "Rhys?" She threw her arms around him as he stood to greet her. "It is so good to meet you. I inherited a brother!"

Rhys grinned as he stepped back. "And I inherited a sister. I could use an extra since I only have one."

My sister loved that and burst out laughing. "Well, I'll leave you guys to dinner. I'm meeting a friend here," she explained. Glancing at me, she added, "I swear I didn't know you'd be here."

Phoebe laughed. "We know that because we decided at the last minute."

Just then, one of my high school teachers came walking in. Tiffany looked his way, and I immediately sensed her tension. He'd been her teacher as well, and she'd loved him. Uncharacteristically, he simply lifted his hand in a wave, his expression guarded but polite. I made a mental note to ask my sister what was going on.

The rest of dinner was uneventful, and I headed back to my place that night with a promise to see Rhys tomorrow for coffee in town. When I got home, I texted Tiffany.

Me: *What was up with Mr. Green tonight?*

Her reply was swift. *Nothing.*

I decided to call. "That wasn't nothing," I said as soon as she answered. "He was your favorite teacher, and you always chat with him."

Tiffany hesitated and then sighed. "You don't know?"

"Obviously, I don't know, or I wouldn't be asking you."

"Mom had an affair with him."

"What? No way."

"Yes, way."

"Oh, for fuck's sake. Who else did she have an affair with?" I muttered.

"Him and that other guy. That's all I know of. I asked Dad and he doesn't know of any others either."

"How did you find this out?" Weariness washed through me. I was so tired of the chaos my mother had left in her wake. Even two years after her death, she was still stirring up shit. I'd respected Mr. Green and was genuinely surprised to learn he'd also fallen prey to her superficial charms.

"His daughter told me."

"Oh, hell," I breathed.

"I know. Remember? He and his wife separated for a while when we were in high school."

"I don't remember that, but then I didn't pay attention to details like that about my teachers." I felt a little sick. "Mom makes me tired, and she's not even here anymore."

"I know. Same," Tiffany replied. "Sorry to share the news."

"It makes me lose respect for him. He and dad were friends."

"I know."

"Does Dad know?"

"I'm not 100 percent sure, but I

think so."

We sat in silence for a moment. What the hell else was there to say?

Tiffany changed the subject. "How did you feel about meeting Rhys?"

"It was good actually. In spite of everything, what Mom lied about, the shock of finding out the way I did, and so on, I like him."

"I thought you would. I was glad to meet him in person finally."

I chuckled. "I'm sure you were."

"Are you going to go to Fireweed Harbor soon to meet the rest of them?" she asked.

"They don't all live there. But, yes, I'm planning to go. Hopefully, I can go soon. I'd like to bring Hallie with me."

"Really?" My sister couldn't hide the excitement in her voice.

"I might as well. They're family too."

"Are you two doing well?" she pressed.

"I think so." I did think so, but I was also traversing entirely new territory in my life—a relationship, a baby and all of the ramifications of that.

Tiffany was quiet for a moment before replying, "I'm glad it's going well. You're going to make an amazing father, Chase."

"I hope so, I really hope so."

Chapter Twenty-Seven

HALLIE

Dr. Williams smiled between Chase and me. "You have a healthy baby boy, and he's right on track."

I took a breath and let it out quickly. "Oh, wow. Okay." I'd been trying so hard to keep my anxiety at bay that I didn't realize how much until the relief rushed through me at hearing good news.

"Just keep doing what you're doing, taking your vitamins and staying healthy. It's all good."

She waved us out, and we scheduled the next appointment. As we walked out, Chase commented, "I've never gone to the doctor this much."

I laughed as I glanced up. "Me neither.

Getting pregnant means a lot of doctor's appointments."

When he smiled, my belly shimmied, and my heart flipped over in my chest. This whole being sensible approach wasn't working. I *really* liked Chase. The only seeds of doubt I had were about whatever family issues Tiffany had implied. I kept reminding myself we all had baggage. I sure did.

I was planning to go to Willow Brook for the weekend. I was even going with him and leaving my car behind. He wanted to bring me back.

As we drove. I looked out at the mountain range nearby with Cook Inlet shimmering under the setting sun. He glanced over, asking, "Have you ever been to Fireweed Harbor?"

"In Southeast Alaska?" I prompted.

"Yeah," he replied, returning his attention to the road ahead.

"Isn't that near Juneau?"

He nodded. "Yep, about an hour away."

"I've only been to Juneau, which is beautiful. Why do you ask?"

I sensed he was nervous, and my emotional radar perked up, wondering if I might get a clue to whatever Tiffany had been talking about.

"So, uh, about two years ago, my sister had us do those DNA tests to see if we had any other family. I learned my father wasn't my biological father. That was one shock, and a few weeks later, I learned about the family I never knew I had."

A little shock jolted through me, and it felt as if my belly was falling for a moment. "Oh, wow. That's some big news."

"I know. Right? I love my dad, and he's my dad in every way that matters and always will be. He said this is just a detail, and it doesn't change how we're a family. But I have seven siblings I never knew about."

"Oh, wow," I breathed.

"I know. It's a lot. I actually had eight, but the eldest one died. Oh, and my biological father passed away before we found this out. Anyway, it's been a process. My mom apparently had a fling with this guy and then ended up marrying my dad. Probably because she thought he was stable and a good option. She didn't know that my bio father was loaded. Ever heard of Fireweed Industries?"

"Of course. They're big news in Alaska. They own that mine everybody was freaking out about until someone new took over."

"Yeah, my cousin. I grew up with him in

elementary school, but we didn't know we were cousins."

"That's a lot to absorb, Chase." I studied his profile. There was a tightness around his eyes.

"Yeah, no shit. Anyway, I've come to terms with it for the most part. My mom hiding it from me is another thing altogether. My half brother Rhys came to meet me last week."

"Oh, you mentioned you had family visiting."

Chase nodded slowly. "I have a standing invitation to Fireweed Harbor, and I thought maybe you'd want to go. I know once we have the baby, travel might be a little more challenging."

I sat quietly for a moment, trying to absorb what this must have been like for Chase. "That's a lot," I offered.

He chuckled and shrugged. "No shit. That seems to be the theme of my life lately."

"I'd love to go," I said firmly.

"You would?" He looked surprised.

"Absolutely. Having somebody with you will take the pressure off."

"You think?"

"Oh, sure. I mean, it's a potentially awkward situation. That would be the case even for people who are prepared." He nodded. "And I'm pregnant, so I'm a great distraction." Chase threw his head back with a laugh. "Do you think it's safe for me to fly?" I belatedly asked.

"I don't know."

"I'll text my doctor right now." I slipped out my phone, tapping out a quick text. "It's to her assistant. She'll read it and let me know." Only moments later, her assistant replied. *You're safe to fly. She said it's better to do it before the last two months of your pregnancy, but it'd be okay then too.*

"How far along are you? Remind me," Chase teased.

I smiled over at him. "You know exactly how far along I am. Five and a half months."

"So we should go soon."

"Just tell me when."

He took a deep breath, his shoulders falling as he let it out. He glanced over just as the exit sign for Willow Brook came into view. "Thank you."

"For what?"

"For offering to go with me. For understanding why it might be good for me to have somebody with me."

He reached across the console, curling his hand over mine where it rested on my thigh and squeezed it. I laced my fingers in his and squeezed back.

This felt good. I was glad he told me what was going on.

We drove in comfortable silence until he turned onto Main Street into Willow Brook and glanced over. "How are you feeling?"

"About what?"

"Us," he said simply.

That single word, *us*, set my heart to pounding in a reckless gallop. My breath was shallow, and butterflies spun in my belly. "Good. I think. What about you?"

He held my gaze for a beat before looking forward at the road. "Good. Really good."

Sometimes with Chase, I felt as if I had jumped off a cliff that I'd been running toward and hadn't known was there. Now, we were falling together. I just hoped our landing would be solid.

CHASE

Hallie was working on her laptop the following morning. She had a glass of juice beside her and was wearing a big fluffy sweater. She was adjusting the color in her photos. I savored watching her work, if only because it felt as if our lives were stitching together more and more.

"By the way, I ran into Jasmine in town. She's looking forward to your help on the marketing for the galleries."

Hallie glanced up with a quick smile. "I am too."

"I'm thinking of hiring some help to finish the house sooner."

Her brows lifted in question.

"I want to have the bedroom ready for the baby," I explained.

Her teeth snagged on her bottom lip as she blinked, her gaze becoming uncertain. I didn't blame her for being nervous. I sure as hell was.

"I guess we should talk about timing. My lease doesn't run out for six months," she offered.

"Okay. I don't want to rush you."

She nodded. After a moment, she looked back at her computer and typed something and then glanced back over. "I had a trip scheduled."

"What do you mean?"

"I used to travel a lot more for gallery showings and contracts for marketing photos. I'm still trying to decide how I'm going to handle that. This was a marketing trip scheduled before I found out I was pregnant."

"Okay." I nodded slowly.

I was worried. This felt like the kind of thing my mom did, bouncing in and out of our lives often. But I didn't say any of that. "How much do you usually travel?"

"I used to travel for months at a time. It's only been in the last year or two that I've mostly been in Alaska."

I nodded again, feeling ridiculous as I just stood there with my hand resting on the counter.

"I thought I'd mention it because I'm trying to figure out what to do about those plans. That's all."

"You don't have to answer to me."

While Hallie's brother had called Rex to find out about me, I called him to check with her brother about Hallie. The second Rex replied, I realized I'd made a mistake.

"You want me to ask her brother how much she used to travel?" Rex asked, his tone dubious.

That alone cued me to what the hell I was doing. "Never mind. That's fucking ridiculous."

"It is. Just ask her. This is part of being in a relationship," Rex said patiently.

A few minutes later, I sat there wishing I'd told my mom how I felt about her before she passed. My need to please her, to keep things smooth with her, had been a powerful force.

As luck, or perhaps un-luck, would have it, I ran into Mr. Green at the grocery store when I was doing my weekly shopping, and he happened to be in the same aisle as me. Mr. Green had been my favorite high school teacher. He'd taught world history. He'd perfected the balance of being firm, while somehow creating the sense he understood you. I really believed he did. He was kind of a nerd, really into history. He also knew a lot about music and covered the history of rock and roll in his class. Lots of students looked up to him. I never, *never* would have suspected he would have had an affair. And with my mom, of all people.

I would have thought he wouldn't have stooped to that level and wouldn't have violated boundaries in that way. I knew from my sister that the affair was after we had graduated from high school, but it still stained my memories of him.

I'd avoided him pretty successfully ever since I'd found out. This was the first time I'd seen him face-to-face. When he saw me, he dipped his chin and cast a quick smile. "Good to see you, Chase."

I studied him for a long moment before I decided to be honest. If there was one thing I'd learned from my mother's death and what she hid from me, it was that secrets didn't help. Especially not when they were found out later.

"I know you had an affair with my mom."

He studied me quietly for a moment, and I could have sworn I saw a flicker of shame in his gaze. He cleared his throat and nodded. "Biggest mistake of my life. I'm sorry you found out."

"Why? It's the truth."

He took a short breath. "I know. If I could change the past, I would. I'm sure it affects what you think of me."

"Of course, it does. You were married. My mom was married. You were friends with my father."

Mr. Green acknowledged this with a nod. "You have every right to be upset. I broke my own trust."

"What do you mean?"

"I try to live with integrity, and life is messy and complicated. We all make mistakes. That's a big one for me, and I can't repair it. I can say I learned from it."

"What the hell do you mean by that?"

"Jenny and I were in a difficult place at the time. If you ever get married or have a long-term relationship—by that, I mean, a decade or two—you learn that people change. You learn that you have to fall in love with each other again and again as you grow. You learn that commitment truly does mean through the good, the bad, and so on and so forth. There are good years and challenging years. Sometimes, the grass looks greener. Clichés become clichés because they tend to be accurate. I made a huge mistake, and I regret it deeply," he said solemnly.

"How does Jenny feel now?"

"I'm still working to regain her trust."

"That was five years ago," I pointed out.

"I know. I'll spend the rest of my life trying to regain her trust. As for your father, he tells me he's forgiven me, but our friendship will never be the same. If anything, it's because it's hard for me to live with what I did."

"My mom was a bright light." I heard myself saying. It was something my father had said many times.

"She was. And, unfortunately, I feel like I hurt her too."

"What?" I sputtered, confused.

Mr. Green took a deep breath, and I saw his hands tighten where they rested on the handle of his shopping cart. "Your mom was always looking for something, or someone else, to fill the places that felt empty inside. I can only answer for myself, but I never intended for it to be anything more than it was, and that was very shallow. I think your mom was always looking for something more."

"My dad was something more." Bitterness laced every single word in that sentence.

I saw the understanding flickering in Mr. Green's eyes, and it made me angry because that was the understanding that I'd loved about him. "Your dad *was* something more, and he still is. I'm sorry your mom couldn't see it. And I'm sorry I couldn't see far enough ahead to realize the damage I was doing. To Jenny, to your father, to you, to Tiffany, to myself, and to anyone who thought I was better than that. I can only hope someday you'll forgive me."

The surface of my heart stung as if an old scar had been torn. I'd spent too many years trying to get something from my mother, something more. While my sister had become the runner, I'd become the pleaser.

"If you want to keep talking, we can," Mr. Green said.

Just then, someone else turned into the aisle. I shook my head, squaring my shoulders and holding his gaze. "Thanks for being honest."

"You know where to find me if you want to talk more."

That was something he used to say in school. Back then, I could find him in his classroom with the rock and roll posters and world maps from different eras in history decorating the walls.

"Thank you."

I moved past him, trying to ignore the achy throb of my heart. I was tired, weary from the years of coming to terms with my mother's actions, and frustrated with how she still managed to twist me up inside even when she wasn't here.

Chapter Twenty-Nine

CHASE

Even though Hallie's doctor cleared her to fly, we decided to take the ferry to Fireweed Harbor for the trip there and then fly back. Ferry travel was common in the southern part of Alaska. Neither one of us had actually taken the ferry to the southeast part of the state. The route was approximately two days, but we had a cabin to sleep in, and the views were stunning.

I stood beside her at the railing on the deck, watching as the wind blew her brown hair in a swirl. My eyes dipped down to the swell of her breasts and her round belly. I found myself more frequently wanting to slide my hand over that curve. Whenever we slept together, I curled behind her with one palm resting there as if I could protect our baby.

"Look!" she said, pointing.

I glanced ahead to see a group of Dall's porpoises zipping through the water.

"They're so fast! Do you know what they are?"

"Dall's porpoises. I saw them once before when I was out fishing with my dad."

We watched for a few minutes before they disappeared from view. Alaska, being typically generous, also gave us the sight of a humpback whale breaching in the distance and a pod of orcas swimming.

Later the following day, Fireweed Harbor came into view. The sunset was in its early stages. It felt as if the town itself was showing off for me, with the light reflected on the water shimmering with orange, red, and pink. The town was nestled into the mountains. A glacier in the distance was bathed in the colors from the setting sun, the otherworldly blue glittering.

"Oh, wow, it's beautiful," Hallie breathed.

We glanced around as the ferry came to a slow stop. Announcements came over the speaker to direct the passengers. We hadn't brought a vehicle, so Rhys was picking us up at the harbor.

My gut churned with anxiety. I was meeting an entire part of my family that I hadn't known existed until recently. The main part of downtown was visible from the harbor as we walked onto the docks. Hallie was ever practical and had a backpack, just as I did, for the weekend.

There were whimsically painted storefronts, cars lining the streets with winding roads that led up the hillside from the main section of town. We walked from the docks into the parking area. I glanced around, turning when I heard my name.

Rhys stood on the sidewalk, waving at us. My anxiety eased a little. I knew him. I just had to meet four more siblings. I supposed I was grateful that two of them were out of town for now, so it wasn't as overwhelming.

I reached for Hallie's hand. Rhys met us halfway, smiling down at Hallie.

She glanced up at him. "You look like Archer," she observed, having met Archer on one of her weekends in Willow Brook.

Rhys grinned. "You must be Hallie."

"I am," she returned. She looked from him to me. "Wow. You two look a lot alike, different eye colors, though."

He grinned before shifting his focus to me. For a second, we hesitated before he pulled me into a back-slapping hug and then stepped back. "Good to see you again. You two ready to go?"

"Sure thing," I replied.

"They're coming in shifts," he said as we got in the car.

"What do you mean?" Hallie asked.

"Well, McKenna's already at the house," Rhys began.

"She's your only sister, right?" I prompted.

"Yours too," he replied.

"It's gonna take a while for me to get used to that."

"I bet." He chuckled. "For now, it's me, McKenna, Adam, and Blake this weekend. We figured we could have dinner at my mother's house."

"I'm good with faces but not so great with names, so I hope everyone's patient with me. I think I can handle three, though," I offered.

Rhys threw his head back with a laugh at that. "Good. Mix them up."

"Who's the youngest again?"

"McKenna, and she hates it. We're stairsteps."

"I thought, if you want, we could go to the main offices tomorrow, and you can check out the business."

"Ooh, where the winery started?" Hallie asked.

"You got it." He glanced over his shoulder, casting a smile at Hallie.

"I've always loved the wine from there, but I can't have any of it now."

"We have non-alcoholic versions of everything, the mead, wine, and beer."

"Oh, wow. I didn't know that."

Rhys shrugged, adding, "We don't distribute those as widely, but it's an option. Plus, there are all the food options too."

"My parents love ordering from there for the holidays," Hallie commented.

"Our holiday gift baskets are legendary."

"But you do so much more now, right?" I prompted.

Rhys nodded. "Oh, yeah. We call the main location in Fireweed Harbor the flagship, but it's basically the family pet project at this point. They expanded fast when they started making money."

Stress churned inside. I didn't know why. It almost felt like I was betraying my father by having a biological father who turned out to be wealthy. I kept those thoughts to myself, though. That wasn't what this weekend was about.

Chapter Thirty

HALLIE

I glanced over at Chase. He looked anxious, irritable, and guarded all at once.

"This is a nice place, but not too ostentatious," I commented.

Rhys had taken us on a tour of the main house before delivering us to a guesthouse on the property. The guesthouse had a living room, kitchen, and bathroom with laundry downstairs. The space was an open concept with a wide stairway to one side that led to a loft upstairs. The loft had an open area with chairs with a view through the floor-to-ceiling windows. Just off that was a bedroom and bathroom. The bathroom was luxurious, with a large oval-shaped tub and a rainfall shower surrounded by glass.

Chase and I were sitting downstairs in a small dining nook in the kitchen. The refrigerator was stocked for us. He glanced over as he ran a hand through his hair and leaned back, reaching for the glass of water I'd poured for him a few minutes ago.

"Are you okay?" I asked.

He finished a swallow of water and set the glass down before shrugging. "This is..." He paused and let out a short sigh.

"This is a lot," I offered. "A lot" had become shorthand between us. I'd originally said it about my unexpected pregnancy and our baby and everything that came with it.

He cracked a half-smile, nodding. "Yeah, it is. I have seven half siblings that I didn't know about and another who passed away."

"I'm so sorry about that," I offered. "Do you know what happened to him?"

"Rhys told me he died of alcohol poisoning in college. He said he was a heavy drinker and a big partier. I get the sense there's more to the story than that." Pausing, he gave his head a little shake. "It's still so weird that Archer is my cousin. We were in elementary school together, and then he moved away."

"Did his family move back here?"

"Yup. His parents ran the Cannon Mine

before it closed. It was about to be re-opened, but Archer took over, and he's renovating all the operations into renewable energy."

I nodded before asking, "How can I help this weekend?"

Chase leaned over, curling his hand over mine. "Just you being here is good."

"I'm great with social chatter. I have to schmooze all the time when I do gallery openings. That'll be my job this weekend."

"Thank you." He turned my hand over, lifting it and dropping a kiss in the center of my palm. The touch was brief, but it felt as if a pebble dropped and sent ripples of heat shimmering through me.

A little while later, we walked from the guesthouse back to the main house. We were expecting to meet McKenna. Rhys had texted that she had come home from running errands and was cooking dinner for all of us this evening. Their mother was out of town this weekend, so it wasn't as many people as I'd worried about on Chase's behalf.

Following Chase's knock, Rhys opened the door a minute later, saying, "You don't need to knock. Our house is yours."

"Not really," Chase corrected.

Rhys didn't miss a beat. "No, really."

We walked into the space, and I glanced around. The space was open, airy, and beautiful. He'd explained earlier that his mother had worked with Archer to update the home to run entirely off renewable power.

He led us down a wide hallway into a kitchen and dining area. A woman was standing at the counter. Her hair was up in a bun with tendrils falling around her face. She and Rhys shared the same silver-gray eyes and dark blond hair.

She rounded the counter, practically skipping. She stopped in front of Chase and threw her arms around him in an enthusiastic hug. Her energy was warm and infectious. He was smiling when he stepped away. "Hey, you must be McKenna."

"Yep. I'm the only woman." She let out a sigh. "I am *so* happy to meet you in person and not just chatting in messages. You have no idea. I finally get a brother who didn't tease me relentlessly when we were growing up."

Chase chuckled, and they fell into a light conversation. After that introduction, two more half-brothers arrived, Blake and Adam. While Chase shared his dad's coloring by coincidence since his mother had the same coloring as well, his features were of the mold of his siblings. The men had chiseled jawlines and angled cheekbones, while McKenna shared the same lines although they were a touch softer.

They were all warm and welcoming. I could sense the undercurrents of uncertainty running through the room. Under the best of circumstances, this was an unusual way to find each other. Chase seemed glad to have me there. I could ask questions and be curious without the burden of wondering if I was crossing some imaginary line.

Later that night after we had returned to the guesthouse, I had asked if he wanted to watch TV. He readily agreed, and I thought he might crave the distraction from, well, everything.

Once we were relaxed on the couch with a show on, I glanced over. "How are you?"

When his gaze met mine, his eyes were tired. "Good. Like you said, it's a lot."

His arm was curled over my shoulders, and he squeezed his palm lightly on my upper arm as if he were trying to reassure me.

"They seem to be trying to keep it low-key."

"I know. Thank god," he said, letting out a sigh. "Thank you."

"For what?"

"For coming with me. You're a good buffer."

I smiled, leaning up to press a kiss on his cheek. Just then, the baby kicked in my belly. Because I was curled up into his side, Chase felt it. We looked down together.

His voice held a hint of wonder in it. "Wow. He's getting busy."

"I told you he's been kicking more."

I felt his knuckles under my chin, and I lifted my gaze to his again, losing myself in the dark heat banked in his. We started kissing, and I forgot any worries tumbling about in my thoughts. The weekend passed quickly. There was only one tense moment that rankled me.

Chase was talking to Rhys, Adam, and Blake. I didn't know what they were talking about, obviously, but he looked over at me. Afterward, he was quiet.

"Everything okay?" I prompted after Rhys dropped us off at the airport.

"Yeah, fine," he said quickly.

I knew this was an emotionally intense weekend for him, so I wasn't going to press, but it stung a little that he wouldn't discuss whatever he was thinking.

Chapter Thirty-One

CHASE

"Come on, Dad. You must have some idea."

My dad eyed me from across the table where we sat in his kitchen. I'd stopped by late one morning to have coffee with him before going into the station.

"Son, you know I would tell you if I knew."

"You didn't tell me about this." As soon as I spoke, I knew those words weren't fair.

He closed his eyes, but not before I saw the pain in them. When he opened them again, his gaze was weary and resigned. "I didn't tell you because I didn't actually *know*. Maybe I had my suspicions, but I didn't believe it was worth kicking up a fuss over something I didn't know. *I* raised you. You're my son. None of this changes my love for you."

"I'm sorry, Dad. I shouldn't have said that," I said quickly. "It doesn't change how I feel about you." I paused, taking a healthy gulp of coffee. "Did you ever wonder if she had another child?"

"Son, I can guarantee you that your mother did not have another child after she had your sister. Even if she had an affair, we were never apart for nine months. I think you're inviting trouble by wondering things like that."

I knew he was right. "I still can't believe she hid this from me. Apparently, she was involved with my bio dad off and on for a year."

"Your mom was like a firecracker." My eyes widened, and he shrugged. "That was your mom. She was exciting, bright, and hard to look away from when things were good. But if you got too close, you got burned. I didn't know who she dated before we met. I knew she had a boyfriend from a summer job. She blamed the breakup on him."

"It sounds like he's the one who called it off," I said flatly. "He caught her cheating on him."

"Makes sense," my dad interjected practically. He cocked his head to the side, studying me. "Chase..." He let out a heavy sigh. "You need to come to peace with what you don't know about your mom. This will eat you up inside. I'm sorry. All I wanted to do was be a father to you and make sure you had a good life."

"You did, Dad. You did. It's just—"

"I know. Your mom was not easy. I never knew how to fix that part of everything. I just kind of let it drift because anything else seemed worse. I wanted her around for your sake."

"So it didn't hurt you that she was always...?" I pressed, not stating the obvious fact she was so often bouncing in and out of our lives..

He shrugged. "At first, I wanted your mom to want to settle down. I eventually just saw it for what it was. She wasn't one to stay in one place."

"What about you and Mr. Green?"

"Yeah, that burned. Not because of your mom, but because of him. Yet I even understood how he ended up in that situation. In his case, he was older and going through a rough patch in his marriage. I'm sure she made him feel on top of the world."

I knew how my mother's attention could feel. It was bright and all-encompassing when it was positive. The shade cast in the aftermath was cold and created a sense of loss.

"I know you're right," I finally said. "I'm working on coming to terms with it."

"How's Hallie?" my dad asked.

My smile came automatically. "She's good."

"How are things working out with you two?"

"Good, I think. I don't know if this is the right approach. I didn't know what else to do. We're having a baby together. If we have a chance at a relationship, it seems we might want to figure that out sooner rather than later." My dad nodded. "I'm just hoping it works out."

"Chase, just be careful."

"About what?"

"You're having a baby together. Your baby is far more important than anything else."

My heart ached through several beats as I realized he wasn't just talking about Hallie and me. He was talking about the choice he made when my mom told him she was pregnant with a baby—me—who turned out not to be his. But he made the commitment before I was even born, and he'd kept it. That was the man he was.

"I know, Dad."

"I love you, son." He reached across the table to clap me on the shoulder and squeeze firmly.

"I love you too, Dad."

My dad was usually right, and I knew he was spot-on about my mom. I couldn't dwell on it. I needed to learn to keep my tangled emotions around my mom from getting in the way of being a father and being a partner to Hallie.

I thought I had it all figured out.

————

Hallie was coming to Willow Brook more often. She liked being around Jasper. He loved resting his chin on her round belly. Hallie was beautiful in a soft, quiet way. Pregnant, she fairly glowed as if illuminated from within. I'd never thought myself the kind of guy to get all mushy. I kept telling myself to be gentle with her, but that just wasn't how it went for us. Once our hands were on each other, we couldn't get enough of each other.

Time and again, after moments of fierce intimacy ticked by, she'd be resting on the pillows, her cheeks flushed pink and her eyes hazed with passion in the aftermath. She looked luminous. Lately, she thought she looked frumpy. Whenever she tried to zip her winter coat, she'd frown down at her round belly.

"You're beautiful," I assured her one morning.

She rolled her eyes. "Thank you. I didn't even have to train you."

I laughed. "Do you want to come into town with me?" I asked. I had to run by the station because I was on call for the weekend and I'd forgotten my on-call bag.

"If you don't mind, I'll just wait here."

"Of course not. I won't be long."

I wasn't. I returned roughly half an hour later, walking in to hear the tail end of a phone call.

"I'm so glad everything's going well. I'd love to be there. Oh, you're coming here? That is awesome. Tell me when, and I'll meet you at the airport if you need a ride."

I couldn't help but be curious. It was my old habit, the eavesdropping habit.

"We're doing really well." I heard her say. There was a moment of silence, and then she said, "Miss you, love you. Take care."

I couldn't help it, but I knew I'd fucked up the second the words came out of my mouth. I toed off my shoes and hung up my jacket, commenting, "You know I've never heard anybody telling a friend they love them."

Hallie set her phone on the counter and turned around. "Excuse me?"

"Just an observation," I added, trying to ignore the stab of uncertainty.

"I told you, Jonathan is one of my best friends. If you're worried, that's ridiculous. He's happily married to his husband."

I was still feeling a little stubborn on this point. "Yeah, but you love him."

"Like a *friend*. I tell my friends I love them. Just because you don't do that doesn't mean other people don't." Her eyes narrowed. "What is your problem with this?"

"Nothing," I said quickly.

It was just all of these conversations sounded so much like the conversations my mom had when she was looking for another way out, a job, a new friend who would last a matter of weeks, the affair I knew about when I was younger, on and on. I didn't tell Hallie that.

"Look, Jonathan is my friend, and he's been in my life a lot longer than you have. If you're going to have a problem with him, then that's a problem for me," she said pointedly.

We stared at each other, and I shrugged,

not really meaning it when I said, "Fine. Understood."

"He's my friend. There's nothing there."

"Yeah, but didn't you try to date?" I pressed.

"Yeah, we tried. Once. We immediately realized it was a bad idea. That was years ago in high school before he came out. Oh, my god. Are you jealous?"

I was. I fucking was, and I didn't want to admit it. I shook my head.

Hallie wasn't having it. "You know what? This is a line for me. I think we should back off. I can't deal with jealousy. You can meet Jonathan, and you can read all of my text messages. Here." She lifted her phone off the counter and held it out. "Read whatever you want. You know my password. I don't have anything to fucking hide. You can ask anybody anything about him. I do love him as a friend, and he's important to me. I don't know what your deal is around this, but you need to figure it out."

Before I could scramble together a rational, reasonable response, Hallie spun around. She strode quickly up the stairs. She was back down in a flash, zipping her backpack. "I was leaving in a few hours, but I think I'll leave now. You're still welcome to come to any doctor's appointments. We'll figure this out. But in the meantime, we'll be friends. Nothing more."

"Hallie," I began.

She held a palm up. "No. I need you to respect me on this. This is important to me."

And then, she was gone.

I banged around the house, my stomach constantly feeling as if I were falling from a great height. My heart clanged in a confused, angry beat, uncertain whether I was angry with myself or Hallie.

A few hours later, she sent me a text. *Here's Jonathan's phone number. Feel free to call him. Here's his husband's phone number. Feel free to call him too. You can ask all the questions you want.*

I felt sick. I had to find a way back out of the mess I'd made. I took a deep breath, startled when the phone rang only minutes later. I snatched it off the coffee table quickly, hoping it was Hallie. Coward that I was, I hadn't had the nerve to call her yet. It was Rhys. I needed a distraction, so I answered.

"Hello."

"Hey there. How's it going?"

"Okay. You?" I replied, my tone clipped.

"Good. Look, I know that conversation about our dad and your mom was a little weird, but I wanted to follow up." I'd already learned Rhys did not waste time.

Today was *that* kind of day, so I took a breath, letting it out before replying, "All right. What's up?"

"She did get pregnant before she had you, but she had an abortion," Rhys said matter-of-factly.

"Oh, uh, okay."

"I figure this whole thing is pretty uncomfortable, so I didn't want to let it hang out there unknown. I had the investigator who helped us locate you look into that."

"I appreciate that," I finally said.

We sat in silence for a minute.

"You okay?" he asked.

"Yeah, I'm fine. We don't need to dwell on this awkward topic."

"Fair enough. How's Hallie?"

My heartbeat felt empty and echoey in my chest. "She's fine."

"Good. We'd love to have you both for a visit again, although I'm guessing travel for her isn't the best plan. McKenna wants to visit Willow Brook. Is that all right with you?"

"Of course."

"Your sister invited her to stay with her," Rhys added.

I chuckled. "That's Tiffany. She's welcome to stay with me as well, although I don't have a ton of space. My main house is under construction."

Tiffany had recently made the decision to move back to Willow Brook and rented an apartment downtown even though she wasn't fully back yet. "I'll let McKenna know. She'll stay in touch with you about when she's coming."

"Awesome. Thanks."

"I should be able to come up next month," he added.

"That'd be great."

We chatted about the weather and timing before ending the call. Afterward, I stared at my phone.

"Wow," I muttered to myself. What could have been a tangled complication wasn't.

I slid my thumb across the screen and pulled up Hallie's phone number, calling her while my heart cast out beats of hope. She didn't answer.

Chapter Thirty-Two

HALLIE

I stared at the screen on my phone, torn between whether to answer or ignore it. I was still frustrated, still uncertain about what to do with Chase, so I ignored it. As soon as it stopped ringing, my heart ached a little. I was tempted to lift the phone and call him right back. I didn't.

The phone rang again, and a little spurt of anticipation zinged through me. I hoped it was Chase again. It was Jonathan. This one, I decided to answer.

"Hey, hey, what's up?" he asked. "You texted."

Oh, god, I had. "I don't know what to do about Chase."

"I thought things were going well."

"They were, but he doesn't understand my friendship with you because we went on one date."

"Ugh. He's being a dumbass. We couldn't even kiss. Does he know that?"

"Yes. You're my best friend, and I don't think he quite gets that part."

Jonathan let out a soft sigh. "Right. He's a straight guy. Sometimes, they're stupid."

"Really?"

"Not to be stereotypical, but yes. And I'm the stereotypical gay best friend."

I burst out laughing. "You're not to me."

"I know, but society thinks I am. Do you love him?"

"I do. But it's all happened so fast. And I'm pregnant. That seems to complicate it."

"Or simplify it," he pointed out.

"How the hell does an unplanned baby, a freaking miracle baby really, simplify anything?"

"Sometimes big things are clarifying."

"What do you mean?"

"Just that this *is* a big thing. Look, new relationships, especially ones that get serious fast, can be overwhelming. That's a fact. Then sorting out each others' pasts can be even more overwhelming. What are his relationship past like?"

"He hasn't had a serious relationship. There's some baggage with his dad and his mom who passed away."

"What has he told you about her?"

"Not much of anything. His sister has implied there's some stuff."

"Stuff?" Jonathan teased lightly. "Well, why don't you ask her? Or, better yet, ask him."

I grumbled, and my friend laughed. "Look, I am not an expert at relationships. I've only had one serious one, and I married the guy. But the most important thing is communication. You're going to have good days and bad days. You're going to have uncomfortable topics, but if you avoid them, you're never going to solve them. There may not even be anything to solve, but you have to be able to talk about it. What exactly happened?"

"He overheard me saying I love you to you when we were finishing up a call. He seemed uncomfortable about it. I got stressed, I guess."

"You guess?"

I rolled my eyes. "Yeah. I guess, and that's

it. I told him we should take a break. I think we should until he can stop being a dumbass."

Jonathan chuckled. "Brilliant. Well, I think you should tell him you'd like to talk. We have been best friends for years, and we tried to date. That didn't work out for obvious reasons, but it might be intimidating. Chris had to get used to my friendship with you."

"What do you mean? How come you didn't mention this to me?"

"I never went into it because it didn't matter to us. He was confused that we tried to date and stayed close. You're still my best friend. Chris is a different kind of best friend."

"I don't know what you mean."

"I know. You will know what I mean someday."

"This feels all very cryptic, Jonathan."

He burst out laughing. "I'm not being cryptic. Call him, or better yet, go see him. Tell him you want to talk. And yeah, tell him to stop overreacting. It's not unusual for him to need to sort out what it means to fall in love with someone who has a best friend that she once tried to date. That's part of figuring a relationship out. I'll be up there next month. That's why I was calling, aside from your text."

"Oh, you will?"

"That's the plan. Chris will be with me. We're planning to move back sometime after the baby is born, so we want to scout out real estate options."

"Oh, wow. This is starting to feel really real."

"I know."

"I'm so happy for you, Jonathan," I said, my heart swelling with emotion.

"I am too. I'm happy for you, and you're going to figure out this thing with Chase."

"I'm starting to wonder if it wasn't the best idea for Chase and me to try to date while I was pregnant."

"There's no great time. You're having the baby, so you might as well figure it out now."

"That's what Chase said."

"Well, he's on point," Jonathan pointed out. I laughed softly. "I hope I get to meet Chase when I'm up there," he added.

"That would be really nice. Text me with an update for when you'll have time to get together next weekend."

"I will. That gives you a week to get your shit together. Miss you."

A laugh slipped out. "Miss you too."

I looked down at the phone again. I was about to call Chase back, but I needed to call my sister-in-law first. Risa was always clear-eyed.

Chapter Thirty-Three

CHASE

I was in the grocery store. Again. This time, I'd run out of coffee, so it was a quick trip. When I rounded the corner and saw Mr. Green standing in front of the coffee, my gut churned. He was a reminder of my mother and her habits. It grated at me that she'd shredded the respect I'd once had for my old teacher. He looked up, and for a second, I thought he was going to turn away. But he turned to face me, sliding one hand in his pocket while the other rested on the handle of his cart.

I tightened my grip on the basket I held, pausing in front of him. "Hi."

He dipped his chin before leveling his

gaze with mine, his eyes studying me. "I've been thinking."

Fucking great.

"I deeply regret what happened with your mother, but I want you to understand something. People screw up. Kids screw up. Adults screw up. We *all* screw up. Life gives us one opportunity after the other to try to get it right. I ran into your father." I nodded. "He mentioned you're struggling."

I rolled my eyes. "I'm surprised you guys are still friendly."

"What happened definitely hurt our friendship. Maybe we can get to the other side of it. Maybe not. I just want you to understand that your mom was always looking for something." I nodded again. "I don't know if she ever found it. Her light shined bright. It was hard to look away from when it was focused on you. This isn't about me asking for your forgiveness, but I hope you can find a way to let go of how your mother's choices affected your life. Because you can't ever change it. She's gone. Maybe you can understand it, and maybe that'll help you let go.

I am *so* sorry. For what my choices meant for my marriage, for my friendship with your dad, and for the way you look at me. It's changed what I think of myself." My breath was shaky as I took in his words. "I suppose I'm saying this because I hope you'll find a way to let things go. Not for anyone other than yourself and whomever you love. I understand congratulations are in order. You're going to be a father."

My throat felt swollen, and I took a slow breath. "Thank you."

"You're a good man, and you have an amazing father. You'll be an amazing father. I know this."

"Thank you." I heard myself saying, my voice husky.

He reached out, squeezing my shoulder, something he had done back when I was a student in his class.

"Thank you for listening. It is what it is. You'll make your own mistakes, and you'll wonder why, and you'll wish it was different. We all have lessons to learn, and sometimes, the things we think will never happen do. There's a difference between forgiveness and letting go. Both are more for you than the other person."

I was able to take a deep breath before he smiled slightly. "I'm sure I'll see you around."

I watched him go and got my coffee and left. As I drove home a few minutes later, I realized he had earned back some of the respect I feared he'd lost forever. Like my dad, he was dealing with the difficult, messy stuff and facing it.

Now, I needed to do it for me, for Hallie, and for our baby boy. I thought about calling her that night, but I wanted to have this conversation face-to-face. That was more important. I sent her a text.

Me: *I'm thinking about you, and I love you. I hope everything's going well. If it's okay with you, I'd like to see you so we can talk.*

I hoped she would reply, but she didn't. I started to get worried when she hadn't replied the next morning either. I called, but she didn't answer. Just when I was about to give up and decided I needed to drive to Anchorage, my phone rang. I didn't recognize the number, but I answered anyway.

"Hello?"

"Hi, Chase?" a man said. "This is Darren, Hallie's brother. I'm calling to let you know she's at the hospital."

"What?"

Chapter Thirty-Four

CHASE

I was speeding. A lot. I couldn't get my heart to slow down with my pulse racing at a full gallop. Dread coated my stomach.

I practically skidded to a stop in the hospital parking lot in Anchorage, bolting through the doorway at the emergency entrance. I stopped at the desk, barking out, "Hallie Thomas."

The receptionist was on the phone. She glanced up, holding up a finger, and I wanted to scream at her.

"Chase?" a voice said.

I glanced around, my eyes landing on a man. Although he was a guy, he looked like Hallie's brother. He shared the same bone structure in his face. He was also wearing his police uniform. He stood from a chair, and I crossed over to him.

"How is she?"

"She's fine." He held a hand out. "I'm Darren."

I distractedly shook it. "I'm Chase. What happened?"

"She slipped."

"What do you mean she slipped?"

A woman approached with two paper cups in her hands. Her dark hair fell in a swingy bob. Her blue eyes were bright and alert as she glanced back and forth between us. "You must be Chase. I'm Risa," she said with a warm smile.

"Yes," I ground out. "I need to know what happened to Hallie."

"I told you. She's fine," Darren repeated.

I took a breath. I wasn't going to feel okay until I could see her. Just then, Hallie's doctor appeared, the very one I'd met when I'd gone to Hallie's appointments with her. She didn't even bother with the niceties. "She's stable," she said before I could even get a word out.

"She is?" I pressed.

"Yes," Dr. Williams replied.

"We both told him that," Risa said, her tone dry.

"Is the baby okay?"

Dr. Williams nodded. "Absolutely fine. We're going to keep Hallie here tonight for observation, but that's solely out of an abundance of caution."

I let out a breath, my chest loosening for the first time since I'd answered the phone and heard Darren's voice. "When can I see her?"

"We're getting her situated in a room right now. You can go back in about ten minutes," the doctor replied.

I nodded, relieved I happened to be standing beside a wall when I sagged against it.

"Sit." Risa herded me over to a chair with Darren and the doctor following. "Do you want some coffee?"

At my nod, she said, "You can have this one. I'll go get another in a minute. I haven't taken a sip from it yet." She handed me one of the cups she held and sat down across from me beside Darren.

"What happened?" I asked.

"She was leaving her studio and slipped on a wet patch on the sidewalk and fell. She started having contractions," Risa explained.

"She fell harder than normal because she has extra weight on her," the doctor offered matter-of-factly. "I'm going to go check on her and make sure she's all situated. When I come back out, you'll be able to go see her."

"Okay. That's it? Are you sure she's okay?" I asked again because it seemed I couldn't ask enough.

"She's fine. She's got some bruising on her back and elbow, but that's it."

After the doctor disappeared, I leaned my head against the wall for a moment, straightening before I took a swallow of the coffee. The bitter flavor jolted me.

"How is it?" Risa asked.

"Okay."

"Could be worse, I suppose," Darren chimed in.

"So how are you and Hallie doing?" Risa asked.

"I was a dumbass," I offered bluntly.

Risa nodded. "You were. Jonathan's harmless and a great guy. You know, they only tried to date once, and they couldn't even kiss."

If I'd been wondering if Hallie discussed what had happened, now I knew. I took another swallow of coffee before replying, "I know. I've never had a friend like that."

"What about your sister?" Risa pressed.

"She's my sister."

"I know, but think of Jonathan like her brother except they don't argue much," Darren offered with a chuckle. "Hallie and I mostly get along, but we had our spats growing up. They didn't."

Resting an elbow on my knee, I nodded. "That makes sense. I was worried when she didn't reply to my texts last night."

Risa shrugged. "Jonathan's coming up to Anchorage next month with his husband. They're planning to move back."

Darren cast a considering look in my direction. "Be a good time to sort shit out."

I bit back a sigh. "I was planning to apologize and tell Hallie I was a dumbass."

"Good, plenty of time for that," he returned with a grin.

I laughed, but it faded fast. "Have you seen Hallie yet?"

"We saw her before she went back for the X-ray on her elbow," Risa replied.

"So I hear you're working on a house," Darren commented.

"I've been doing it piecemeal because I live in a smaller place on the property, but I want to hurry it up."

"If you want some help, I'll come up on weekends," he offered.

"You will?"

"Sure, I'm handy. I promise I won't screw anything up."

"He built an addition on our house," Risa interjected.

"I'll take all the help I can get. I have some friends who have been helping on the weekends too. Maybe we can make some serious progress. The outside is done. I just need to finish the inside."

"Say the word, and I'll be up on the weekends," Darren replied with a firm nod.

"That would be awesome."

"If Hallie's out of here tomorrow, I'll start coming up this weekend. How long do you think it will take?"

"I figure with extra help, maybe four or five weekends."

"Let's get it done."

"Wow. That's a big help. Thank you."

Darren chuckled. "It's selfish. I want my sister to have space for the baby. She doesn't at her apartment."

Just then, the doctor appeared, waving me over. "I'll be back." I stood and followed her down the hallway.

She stopped in front of a door. "She's settled and comfortable. She knows you're here."

When I walked through the door and saw Hallie in the bed, my heart felt like a jack-hammer in my chest, and my eyes stung with tears.

Chapter Thirty-Five

HALLIE

Chase closed the door behind him. His eyes were pinned to me as he crossed the room.

"Hey," he said, his voice gruff. His hand curled over mine where it rested beside my hip. "How are you feeling?"

"I'm fine." I *was* fine, and I was annoyed at my situation. My elbow was sore, and this whole thing had been an ordeal. "All I did was fall. I wouldn't even be at the hospital if I wasn't pregnant." I smoothed my free hand over my belly.

He rested his other hand over mine. Just then, as if to make a point, our baby kicked. Chase leaned down, pressing a kiss to my temple before straightening. His eyes skated over my face.

"I'm sorry, and I'm a dumbass."

"You're not a dumbass."

"I'm not?"

"Well, no, but maybe yes."

"I overreacted."

"You need to get used to Jonathan being a part of my life. He's my best friend."

"I know. Our relationship is fresh, and it's a lot. I overreacted," he repeated.

"Is it all that simple?"

"I don't know. We're figuring it out a day at a time, right?"

"We are," I replied.

He squeezed my hand. "Are we okay?"

I smiled up at him. "I missed you."

"I love you," he whispered.

" I love you too." My voice was raspy, and the words were true with my heart thumping in recognition.

He leaned down, brushing his lips over mine. Our baby kicked again, and I felt the curve of his smile before he straightened. "The doctor says you're going to be here for the night. Can I stay?"

"I don't know. Where's Jasper?"

"I asked my dad to pick him up for the night before I left. I met Darren and Risa."

"Oh?"

"He told me to stop being a dumbass."

"Ah, I talked to Risa, and she probably told Darren," I explained.

"He said if things were okay with us, he would come up to help me finish the house on the weekends."

"Really?"

Chase nodded. "What do you think about that?"

"It'd be nice. I mean, we don't have room at my apartment. We have room at your smaller place, but we'll want more space in the long run. If Darren's volunteering to help, I say take him up on it. He did an addition on their house, and it looks great."

"I trust him," Chase replied. His eyes dipped down, coasting over me. "How's your elbow?"

"It's sore, but that's it. My back is a little sore, but it's not bad."

"You're not allowed to fall again," he ordered.

"I'll try not to," I replied with a grin.

I wanted time alone with Chase, but that didn't really work out. Risa and Darren came to the room for a visit. Nurses came to check on me on a schedule, and there was a constant flow of beeps and other sounds in the background. But he slept in a chair beside my bed. He refused to get in the bed with me because he said it was too narrow. He was worried he'd hurt my elbow or the baby.

It didn't matter. It felt so good to have him there.

Chapter Thirty-Six

CHASE

Darren kept his word. He began coming to Willow Brook every weekend with the goal to finish the house in time for the baby. As planned, Jonathan and his husband Chris came for a visit to look at real estate in preparation for their eventual move after their baby was born and helped out with a few things on the house as well. Meeting Hallie's best friend only illuminated what an idiot I'd been. He *was* really like a brother to her.

Hallie's due date was a month away, and she sat at the table in the new kitchen. She smiled over at her brother. "Thank you, Darren."

He flashed a grin as he turned and let the

refrigerator door fall closed. "Hey, I was motivated."

Risa chuckled from where she sat beside Hallie. "He likes things to be ready."

Hallie giggled. "I know. He's always been like that."

"Is that a problem?" Darren said as he cracked open the beer he'd just fetched out of the fridge.

"No. It totally benefits me this time," Hallie replied honestly.

He sat down beside me. "I think one more weekend?" he asked, the lilt of a question in his voice.

"You've done more than enough. You don't have to come up again. You guys have been here every weekend for the past month," I said.

"Yeah, but after all this work, I want to see it through," Darren insisted. "I know how busy you are."

"Fortunately, this is a quieter time for me," I replied. "Give it another few months, and I'll be a lot busier."

Darren nodded. "That and the baby will be here."

I was grateful that Hallie's family completely understood my work schedule. I'd never intended to be a hotshot firefighter for the rest of my life. The work was too physically demanding to do long-term. You reached a point when you had to call it quits. But with Darren being a police officer, and Hallie's father a retired one, they understood the commitment and respected it. As it was, I had already told Graham I needed at least a full month off after Hallie had the baby. I wanted to have that time for us and make sure she felt like everything was settled before I got called out to travel for weeks at a time.

"I'm not going to complain. I appreciate everything you've done, and I didn't expect it."

"Well, it wasn't just me," Darren replied.

"Definitely not." Graham, Beck, and a few other friends had been coming by regularly to help. Rhys and Blake had even come out for a weekend. "All I've got left is a punch list for the final details," I commented.

Darren chuckled. "We can knock that out in two days."

Risa had taken it upon herself to help Hallie pick out furnishings. There were a few finishing touches left, but she was as committed as Darren was. As Hallie pointed out, Risa had excellent taste as the manager of several art galleries.

Hours later, after Darren and Risa had gone into the newly furnished guest bedroom, Hallie's palm was resting on her belly where she lay propped up on the pillows. My heart flipped over in my chest when I came out of the bathroom. She set her e-reader to the side and smiled over at me.

"This has turned out to be a handy shelf," she teased as she smoothed her hand over her belly.

Crossing over, I lifted the covers and slid in beside her. "A shelf? It's round."

"Yeah, but the top of it is flat when I'm laying down, sort of."

I leaned on an elbow, facing her and smoothing my hand over the lower curve of her belly. Just then, the baby kicked hard. We both laughed. "That must feel so weird," I said. "I still can't believe you have a mini-human growing inside you."

My eyes met hers, and my heart flipped in my chest again. That often happened when I let myself really *feel* what was happening for me with Hallie and with our baby.

"I know. Thank you," she said, her gaze sobering.

"For what?"

She took a deep breath. "Everything. This was a surprise. We didn't expect to see each other again. You're not only with me in this, but—" Pausing, she gestured around the room. "You've completely finished a whole new house just so we have room for the baby."

"It's what I want."

"I know. It's just I didn't expect this."

"We didn't expect any of this," I murmured. I leaned closer and gave her a lingering kiss. "I want to keep you close. I want all of it. With you. With our baby."

EPILOGUE

Hallie

"Come on. Let's go," Jasmine ordered.

"You can't leave the gallery," I protested.

"Hallie, yes, I can. Your water just broke." She rolled her eyes before grabbing my purse and jacket from the chair beside me.

"But it's three days early," I pointed out. "This isn't how it's supposed to go."

Jasmine ignored my comments. Moments later, she had hustled me into her car, and I called Chase. "My water broke," I announced as soon as he answered.

"Did you call the ambulance?" he sputtered, his usual calm presence rattled.

"I'm with Jasmine. She's taking me to the hospital here, not Anchorage."

"It'll be quicker," Jasmine said loudly enough for Chase to hear.

"She's right," he said. "I'll meet you there."

The next few hours passed in a jumble. All I could remember were slides of it, like those old slideshows when they showed one memory at a time. The car ride where I was surprisingly calm. Arriving at the hospital and being rushed in. Chase getting there moments later. The intense look of love in his eyes. My contractions were sharp, the pain literally snatching my breath out of my chest. Between wasn't that bad. It went more quickly than I'd expected.

Holly, one of the ER nurses and a friend of Chase's, popped in to check on me and let me know she'd called Darren and my parents and that my doctor from Anchorage would be there soon. I had no sense of time and was startled to hear the doctor announce the time of birth.

"It's not even five o'clock," I wheezed after she'd said it was 4:43 p.m.

Chase, who looked worn out and overwhelmed, met my eyes, his lips kicking into a smile. "Yeah, you're really efficient."

My doctor chuckled. "Agreed. The first labor can last longer, but not in your case.

From the time your water broke until now, it's only been four hours and three minutes."

Our baby boy was placed on my chest. I didn't remember falling asleep, but I did. Hours later, I came awake, still utterly exhausted. It was dark, and the lights were dimmed in the room. Chase was sitting in a chair beside me. His fingers were laced through mine with our baby sound asleep on his chest.

I rolled my head to the side.

"Hey," he said softly. "How are you feeling?"

I did a mental scan, reporting, "Sore, but okay."

"He just finished nursing about an hour ago, and I was pretty sure you wouldn't remember waking up. The nurse says he's nursing like a champ."

I shook my head.

"Do you want to hold him?" He carefully shifted the bundle into my arms.

"Oh, wow. He's here," I murmured.

"Wow is one way to put it," Chase said softly, smoothing my hair.

For a moment, our baby boy opened his eyes, and his gaze met mine. I experienced a jolt inside, and a sense of connection shimmered between us. His eyes closed, and I rolled my head to look at Chase again. "Wow," I breathed.

He smiled. "It's three of us now."

Want a glimpse of the future for Hallie & Chase? Join my newsletter to receive an exclusive scene.

Sign up here: https://BookHip.com/DRJFMWA

p.s. If you are already subscribed, you'll still be able to access the scene.

Coming next in the Light My Fire Series is With Every Breath.
Alice's return home to Alaska all starts with putting on an accidental skinny-dipping show for a wedding party. Oops.

Jonah happens to be Alice's new neighbor, and the first time he sees her she's naked.
Well then.

Jonah came to Alaska to escape painful memories. He considers himself damaged goods and not fit for romance. He didn't plan on Alice. He didn't plan on the fire blazing to life between them.

Don't miss Alice & Jonah's story - it's emotional, sexy, sweet and full of heart & soul!

Pre-order With Every Breath - due out Oct 11, 2022!

For more swoony romance...

This Crazy Love kicks off the Swoon Series - small town southern romance with enough heat to melt you! Jackson & Shay's story is epic - swoon-worthy & intensely emotional. Jackson just happens to be Shay's brother's best friend. He's also *seriously* easy on the eyes. Shay has a past, the kind of past she would most definitely like to forget. Past or not, Jackson is about to rock her world. Don't miss their story! Free on all retailers!

Burn For Me is a second chance romance for the ages. Sexy firefighters? Check. Rugged men? Check. Wrapped up together? Check. Brave the fire in this hot, small-town romance. Amelia & Cade were high school sweethearts & then it all fell apart. When they cross paths again, it's epic - don't miss Cade's story!
Free on all retailers!

For more small town romance, take a visit to Last Frontier Lodge in Diamond Creek. A sexy, alpha SEAL meets his match with a brainy heroine in Take Me Home. Marley is all brains & Gage is all brawn. Sparks fly when their worlds collide. Don't miss Gage & Marley's story!
Free on all retailers!

If sports romance lights your spark, check out The Play. Liam is a British footballer who falls for Olivia, his doctor. A twist of forbidden heats up this swoon-worthy & laugh-out-loud romance. Don't miss Liam & Olivia's story.
Free on all retailers!

5) Follow me on Instagram at https://www.
instagram.com/jhcroix/
6) Like my Facebook page at https://www.
facebook.com/jhcroix

———

Visit my store to purchase ebooks & fun swag!
J.H. Croix Shop
Light My Fire Series
Wild With You
Hold Me Now
Only Ever Us
Fall For Me
Keep Me Close
With Every Breath - coming Oct 2022!
Dare With Me Series
Crash Into You
Evers & Afters
Come To Me
Back To Us
Take Me There
After We Fall - coming Aug 2022!
Swoon Series
This Crazy Love
Wait For Me
Break My Fall
Truly Madly Mine

Still Go Crazy
If We Dare
Steal My Heart
Into The Fire Series
Burn For Me
Slow Burn
Burn So Bad
Hot Mess
Burn So Good
Sweet Fire
Play With Fire
Melt With You
Burn For You
Crash & Burn
That Snowy Night
Brit Boys Sports Romance
The Play
Big Win
Out Of Bounds
Play Me
Naughty Wish
Diamond Creek Alaska Novels
When Love Comes
Follow Love
Love Unbroken
Love Untamed
Tumble Into Love
Christmas Nights
Last Frontier Lodge Novels

Take Me Home
Love at Last
Just This Once
Falling Fast
Stay With Me
When We Fall
Hold Me Close
Crazy For You
Just Us

ACKNOWLEDGMENTS

This story was a long time coming in my imagination. Hallie appeared as the hero's sister in Tumble Into Love in the Diamond Creek Series (my first series!), and I always planned to write her story. I kept waiting for her hero to appear for me, and he took his sweet time. I was starting to sweat it. Along came Chase, and I knew he was the man for Hallie. To those readers who asked about her story, thank you for your patience. To all of my readers - THANK YOU!

Gracious thanks to my editor and to Terri D. for her thorough attention to detail. As always, many thanks to my early readers.

Much gratitude to the bloggers, bookstagrammers, and booktokers who share the love of romance, my stories and those of so many authors with the world. My assistant makes it possible for me to focus on my stories and tidies up more details than I can count.

To my husband, my family, and my dogs, also family ;): all my love.

xoxo
J.H. Croix

ABOUT THE AUTHOR

USA Today Bestselling Author J.H. Croix lives in a small town in Maine with her husband and three spoiled dogs. Croix writes contemporary romance with sassy women and alpha men who aren't afraid to show some emotion. Her love for quirky small-towns and the characters that inhabit them shines through in her writing. Take a walk on the wild side of romance with her bestselling novels!

Places you can find me:
jhcroixauthor.com
jhcroix@jhcroix.com

facebook.com/jhcroix

instagram.com/jhcroix

bookbub.com/authors/j-h-croix

www.ingramcontent.com/pod-product-compliance
Lightning Source LLC
Chambersburg PA
CBHW071212210726
48293CB00002B/397